"What do your instincts say now?"

With her upper body pressed down upon Lincoln's chest and a gleam of pure, intense raw desire in his eyes, Bobbie fought for control.

Of her body.

Her desire.

The need to kiss him. Taste him. Have him.

You can't. You can't.

Then Lincoln reached up to free her hair and entwine his fingers through the waves as he pulled her head down to his.

Bobbie gasped softly.

The anticipation was intoxicating and not to be denied.

The first feel of his tongue flicking against her mouth was the beginning and the end of her resistance. Her entire body felt a spark like nothing ever before.

Ever.

She trembled as she tumbled face-first into passion. It was exhilarating. New. Different. Addictive.

"Lincoln," she sighed just before he deepened the kiss with a guttural moan.

Like he was starving for her.

She matched his h_____ m as she succumbe_

An Offer from Mr._____ f the C_____ series.

Dear Reader,

It's time for another of my "Sexy, Funny & Oh So Real" romances. While writing *An Offer from Mr. Wrong*, book three in the Cress Brothers series, I smiled, chuckled and cried. Lincoln, the new eldest son of the Cress family, is fighting for the love of his life—Bobbie, the strong-willed and sexy private investigator—and his place within the high-profile family of wealth and means. I *loved* writing this story so much. Lincoln and Bobbie go from adversaries to allies to friends to lovers and then back to friends before finally welcoming the love. Even with all the ups and downs, in the end, it's worth it—just like a roller-coaster ride.

What's your reading routine? Mine includes a warm drink, a comfy spot, usually a soft blanket and some quiet to get lost in the story—especially an emotional one. And this one is packed with *all the feelings* in the best way. I love it, and after more than twenty years as a writer, I can say its one of my faves. I am so happy it is *finally* ready to be shared with the world.

Here's to hoping you all enjoy the ride.

Best,

N.

NIOBIA BRYANT

—

AN OFFER FROM MR. WRONG

Recycling programs
for this product may
not exist in your area.

ISBN-13: 978-1-335-73574-4

An Offer from Mr. Wrong

Copyright © 2022 by Niobia Bryant

For questions and comments about the quality of this book,
please contact us at CustomerService@Harlequin.com.

Harlequin Enterprises ULC
22 Adelaide St. West, 41st Floor
Toronto, Ontario M5H 4E3, Canada
www.Harlequin.com

Printed in U.S.A.

Niobia Bryant is the award-winning and nationally bestselling author of fifty romance and mainstream commercial fiction works. Twice she has won the RT Reviewers' Choice Best Book Award for African American/Multicultural Romance. Her books have appeared in *Ebony*, *Essence*, the *New York Post*, the *Star-Ledger*, the *Dallas Morning News* and many other national publications. One of her bestselling books was adapted to film.

Books by Niobia Bryant

Harlequin Desire

Cress Brothers

One Night with Cinderella
The Rebel Heir
An Offer from Mr. Wrong

Harlequin Kimani

A Billionaire Affair
Tempting the Billionaire

Visit her Author Profile page at Harlequin.com, or niobiabryant.net, for more titles.

You can also find Niobia Bryant on Facebook, along with other Harlequin Desire authors, at Facebook.com/harlequindesireauthors!

As always, this one is dedicated
to the wonderful thing called love.

One

Over the rim of her flute of champagne, Bobbie Barnett eyed the couple across the restaurant sharing intimate kisses in their booth seating. The champagne chilling in ice, lit candles and strawberry-with-cream dessert were romantic. A Midtown Manhattan restaurant of such quality would offer nothing less.

"Aww so sweet," Bobbie drawled as she used black-framed camera glasses to secretly record them. "Too bad it's not his wife."

When the man's hand dipped beneath the table, Bobbie looked away, sparing herself and his wife from viewing the scandalous spectacle. She was being paid a hefty fee to prove what women's intuition—and probably many late nights spent alone in bed—had already alerted his wife to regarding his infidelity.

The gut never lies.

As a private investigator, Bobbie relied on hers.

She was called upon by wealthy and influential people to solve mysteries, investigate crimes and prove betrayals. She *loved* it—almost as much as her father, Bobby. She'd inherited the business from the PI and former police detective upon his retirement. After being raised from childhood to be observant and inquisitive she became a detective and passed her private investigator test at twenty-five. With twelve years in the game, she was one of the best.

Bzzzzzz.

She flipped her phone over on the table. A text from her client Mrs. Ferguson. "'Any updates?'" Bobbie mouthed, before biting off a bit of her caramel-tinted lip gloss.

She understood the desperation and stress of suspecting a spouse of cheating all too well. Long gone was the anger of discovering her husband, Henny Santana, in bed with another woman. Now hurt remained. It clung to her like a second skin.

For the lost years of her life.

For broken trust.

For feeling foolish in ever believing in him.

With a slight shake of her head that caused the loose waves of her wild hair to bounce, she tapped her glossy almond-shaped nails against the stem of the crystal flute. Pushing aside feelings she fought hard to forget, she raised the glass and took a deep sip of the vintage champagne.

Rehashing my marriage to Henny is a waste of time.

"Speaking of *my* time," Bobbie muttered, checking her phone.

8:28 p.m.

She was killing two birds with one stone. Surveillance for one client and an appointment with a potential new one.

That morning she had closed a case on a missing A-list celebrity whose manager was panicking at unreturned phone calls. Some old-school sleuthing aided by modern-day technology and she learned the actor was tucked away at a luxury hotel recovering from secret plastic surgery to "revitalize" his face. Without revealing the actor's truth, she assured the manager his client was alive and well.

It was a long day and she was ready for a relaxing lengthy bath, meditation and then—hopefully—deep sleep in the middle of her big comfy bed with her crisp sheets pressed against her naked—

"*You're* B. Barnett?"

Bobbie stiffened.

Rarely was she surprised, but the sound of the male voice did just that. She recognized the deep timbre and the British accent.

Lincoln Cress.

She raised her head to look up at the tall and broad-shouldered man with rugged features. Square jaw and chin. Broad nose. Deep-set eyes beneath slashing brows. High cheekbones. Trimmed goatee framing his soft mouth currently diminished by a frown.

A handsome man with an ugly countenance who was no happier to see her than she was to see him.

No matter how fine.

On the edge of her aggravation were awareness and excitement.

Bobbie cleared her throat and offered him the seat

across from her as she crossed her legs. "Nice to meet you, Lincoln," she said as he remained standing.

"Meet me?" he snapped, his face the epitome of annoyance. "You invaded my life for weeks!"

She understood his annoyance.

Last fall, she was hired to investigate Phillip Cress Sr., acclaimed chef and giant in the culinary empire, by two of his five sons, Coleman and Gabriel. She was thorough, even going back to Phillip's days growing up in the small seaside town of St. Ives in Cornwall, England. A perfunctory background check revealed his name on the birth certificate of Lincoln Cress, his illegitimate son born before he met and wed his wife, Nicolette Lavoie.

When the Cress brothers then hired her for an extensive background check of their newly discovered half brother, Bobbie traveled to St. Ives pretending to be a biographer of local England chefs. She found Lincoln to be rude, stiff and intolerant of her attempts to learn more about him for her feigned work. She lost count of just how many times he had escorted her out of his Michelin-starred restaurant.

Foolishly, she'd thought she'd never come face-to-face with the wickedly handsome grouch again.

"If you'd like to have a conversation, I'd prefer you weren't scowling and looking down above me, Mr. Cress," she said, glancing past him to see Mr. Ferguson was busy enjoying his date with his mistress.

Lincoln jerked back the chair and finally folded his towering frame to sit.

A uniformed waiter instantly appeared. "Would you like to start with a drink?" he asked.

"Trust me—what he needs, Kevin, you do not serve," she drawled, picking up her flute.

An enema would change his attitude because he was full of—

"First intrusion and now insults," Lincoln said, his dark eyes locked on her face.

Her curiosity of what he thought of her looks was the second surprise of the night.

Lincoln Cress annoyed her but his presence gave her an undeniable thrill.

"I'll give you some more time," Kevin said before quickly backing away.

"I was hired to do a job," she began, ready to send him and his negative energy on his way. "And since you're here in New York and aware of my involvement I assume you have connected with your long-lost father and half brothers—who are all extremely wealthy. So… you're welcome."

"Is that how you sleep at night? Without conscience or integrity?" he asked.

"And how do you rest on that high horse?" she countered.

"I knew you were up to no good when I first spotted you in my restaurant," Lincoln said.

"Oh," Bobbie said, drawing it out. "O-kay then. So, you want to take it *there*?"

Lincoln shook his head and released a sardonic chuckle. "We were there ever since you invaded my life to spy on me."

"Life is about perspective, Mr. Cress," she began, tracing the rim of the glass with her fingertip. "You could see my role in your life as a negative and intrusive thing…or…be thankful that my actions led to you being reconnected with the father you've never known."

Lincoln's jaw clenched. "I don't need his money," he said, with coldness.

Bobbie held up her hands and nodded. "I know," she said with confidence.

Renewed anger brought a spark to his dark eyes.

"Listen, it was nothing personal for me. It was a job," she explained. "Just like I'm trying my best not to hold a grudge for you being an intolerable butthole toward me."

"You've got a lot of nerve," he drawled, leaning forward to rest his elbows atop the table.

"And you are the epitome of a miserable soul," she snapped, leaning forward to do the same.

Just inches separated them. The scent of the small bouquet on the center of the table wafted up between them as his eyes pierced hers with an intensity that made Bobbie fight not to lick the sudden dryness from her lips. She fought and failed, giving her bottom lip a tiny bite as she leaned back from being so near to him.

When his eyes dropped to her mouth to take in the innocent gesture, her heart pounded.

Fast and hard.

She had felt the same awareness when she first laid eyes on the brute…

Bobbie entered the beautifully rustic seaside restaurant and was drawn in by the charm of the wood interior, teal decor, wild floral arrangements at each table and the scent of fresh seafood cooked in butter, garlic and other flavors. In the center of the intimate space was an open kitchen. Her eyes had sought and found

Lincoln Cress where he was busy giving out sharp orders to his staff.

Her heart skipped a beat and then pounded.

The photo of him from his website did him no justice. It lacked the intensity lining his face as he shifted a pan atop a fiery burner back and forth and then flipped the contents inside it with impressive skill.

And it was surprisingly arousing.

"Welcome to SHORES. I'm Shirly. Can I start you off with a drink or appetizer?"

With reluctance, Bobbie shifted her eyes away from the chef and up at the waitress offering her a welcoming smile as she clutched a small tablet to enter orders. "Actually, I'm Kimberly Madison, a biographer researching local chefs," she lied with ease.

"Oh. The American that's been callin'," the waitress said with a British accent heavy with Cornish dialect.

Bobbie didn't miss that the woman cast a nervous glance back at the kitchen in Lincoln's direction. "I thought reaching out in person to see if he was interested in participating in the project would get me a little further," she said, as she looked down at the paper menu atop the place setting. "And I would love to try the squid."

Shirly gave her a nod and smile before moving away.

Bobbie looked on as the waitress made her way behind the bar to the opening of the kitchen. They shared words before Lincoln leaned his head over to look directly at her. She gave him a warm smile and wave of her fingers.

He glared back in return.

She looked on as he finished something he was cooking and plated it before barking a few orders to the rest of the cooking staff. Her heart pounded as he left the kitchen and moved with long strides toward her. His black chef's coat against his shortbread complexion and slashing brows was eye-catching.

Lincoln Cress was eye candy ready to be devoured—in the best way.

As he neared her, Bobbie's brows raised with each step. The look of annoyance on his face became clearer. She rose to her feet and extended her hand as he came to a stop near her table.

"I already told you I wasn't interested and would appreciate not being harassed," Lincoln said, ignoring her hand as he folded his arms across his chest. "You're annoying."

Bobbie fought the urge to fold her hand into a fist and gut-punch him. "And you're rude," she countered, losing patience with his insolence.

He nodded sharply. "When annoyed? Yes," he agreed.

"When breathing is more like it," she shot back.

"Goodbye," he stressed, widening his eyes with incredulity before lightly touching her elbow and steering her toward the glass front door.

"No. You. Are. Not," she snapped as he gave her a wave before closing the door in her face, leaving her with her mouth still open in shock.

Bobbie frowned at the memory. She couldn't stand the man.

"What do you want from me? I already apologized," she said, thinking of the bath and other relaxation activities she had planned.

"For you to find another occupation where you're not paid to lie, pretend and exploit people who did not choose to have you in their lives," Lincoln said, his eyes raising to lock with hers.

And just like their first meeting, as her heart pounded and her pulse raced, he opened his mouth and threw cold water on the heat building inside her.

Lincoln Cress was an honest man. He prided himself on that. And the undeniable truth was Bobbie Barnett was a beautiful woman. From her wild mane of loose waves that reached beyond her shoulders in length and breadth, to her brown complexion, and the most glorious full lips covered in a sheer brown gloss. Her look was a throwback to the 1970s' Donna Summer vibe and it was hard to deny the allure.

Her allure.

He tapped his index finger atop the restaurant's table as he sat back in his chair and continued to eye her. He recognized her at first sight, but now knew she had lied about who she was when they first met. "Kimberly," he said with snark.

"Bobbie—with an *IE*, not a *Y*," she countered.

It fit. It was a perfect match for her.

"Again, I apologize," she added.

Kevin the waiter reappeared.

"Nothing for me," Lincoln said, his thoughts full.

There had been a lot of changes and discoveries in his life in the last week. The sudden phone call from the man he'd always been told was his father had been shocking enough. His proclaiming to never have known of his existence until a report by a private investigator revealed it to him had truly shaken Lincoln. He had gone through a wide range of emotions before settling on curiosity.

About the father he knew only by name.

About the truth. Every day of his forty-four years his mother declared his father knew about him.

About his siblings after being an only child all his life.

About so much more.

Lincoln got the call and the next day he was on a private jet to New York to meet the world-renowned Phillip Cress and take two DNA tests—an at-home test and then a court-admissible one for confirmation. The next day after that he met Nicolette Lavoie-Cress, Phillip's wife, and his five half brothers.

Five.

Phillip Junior, Sean, Gabriel, Cole, and Lucas.

All younger than him.

And that meeting had been wild.

Lincoln didn't know who was angrier at him: his mother for him agreeing to connect with his father or Phillip Junior for his very existence uprooting him as their father's eldest son.

Bzzzzzz.

He eyed Bobbie as she picked her phone up from the table. She bit her bottom lip and furrowed her arched brows as she began typing with her thumbs. As she stared at the screen awaiting a response, she trailed the tips of her nails across the brown skin exposed by the deep vee of the cream satin tank she wore beneath an olive motorcycle jacket. A soft smile touched her glossy lips as she continued to text. He was reminded of the moment in his restaurant when he looked over at her and she gave him that same smile and a wave.

Her hair had been slicked back into a bun and her

face free of makeup. More subdued. An attempt to be inconspicuous.

She had failed.

A woman like Bobbie Barnett fading into the background?

Impossible.

"You're rude," Lincoln said, feeling a need to point out a bad trait.

She looked up from her phone. "No, I'm busy," she countered setting the phone down and looking over his shoulder as she adjusted her spectacles.

Cha-ching.

When she ignored the newest notification and leaned to the right of him, he looked back over his shoulder and then back at her coolly. "Are you watching that couple?" he asked, his voice cold and judging.

"Mind your business?" Bobbie snapped with a wave of her hand like swatting away a fly.

"Hell, you mind yours," he shot back.

She picked up her phone and turned it to face him to show a transfer of fifteen thousand dollars. "Business pays," she said, signaling for the waiter.

"Anything for money, huh?" Lincoln drawled with derision.

Her face tightened with anger. "Anything to help clients find resolution," she said, her coldness matching his as her eyes lit with the fire of anger. "To help people being lied to and cheated on. To help people scammed in their businesses. To help solve crimes. To protect people. *And* to help families connect with lost family members."

Kevin came to a stop at their table.

"I'm ready for my check," Bobbie said, tucking her

hair behind her ear and exposing more of her large and thin gold hoop earrings.

"I'll be right back with it, Ms. Barnett," Kevin said before leaving them once again.

They stared at one another in stony silence until he returned.

Bobbie stood up and removed a money clip from the side pocket of her cargo pants. She placed cash inside the billfold before handing it to the waiter.

Lincoln rose to his feet as well. He was just over six feet but in her strappy bronze sandals, her eyes were level with his lips. She tilted her head back to look at him, causing the soft waves of her hair to fall back from her face.

She is intoxicating.

They eyed one another. Studied each other.

The loud splash of water echoed followed by horrified gasps.

Lincoln and Bobbie turned their heads in the direction of the melee.

A woman in an elegant strapless dress stood next to the table of the couple Bobbie had been spying on. The gentleman's face and front of his shirt were wet.

Lincoln frowned at the public display. "Ridiculous," he muttered, before looking down at Bobbie—who no longer wore her spectacles.

Her deep brown eyes were bright with just the hint of hazel.

"Your handiwork?" he asked. "Proud of yourself?"

She looked up at him. "For helping a stressed-out wife being gaslit by her cheating husband to believe she's crazy when the whole time she's right about him cheating…*on* the night of their fifteenth anniversary," Bobbie said, her words clipped with her anger.

"Bitter much?" Lincoln snarked.

Bobbie tilted her head to the side and gave him an assessing look. "A chakra cleanse. New outlook on life. Great sex," she said, ticking each off on her fingers.

"Excuse me?"

"The three things you *need* in your life," she said, giving him a slow and thorough once-over. "ASAP."

Lincoln grated his teeth to keep from telling her just how great his sex was. "Stay the hell out of my life, B. Barnett," he said instead, before reclaiming his seat.

Her hand landed on his shoulder.

Lincoln was startled by her touch.

"Careful, you might need my services one day, Mr. Cress," she said.

The soft and warm scent of her perfume clung to her inner wrist. It was intriguing.

Lincoln jerked his head back. "Never," he promised.

"So long forever then," she said.

"Good riddance," he retorted.

And she walked away.

Don't look. Do. Not. Look.

Lincoln did indeed look back. He was rewarded with the sultry back and forth sway of Bobbie's hips in the low-slung cargo pants she wore with heels. He forced his eyes away.

Having snooped into his life, Bobbie Barnett rubbed him the wrong way—sex appeal or not.

"Excuse me. Mr. Cress?"

Lincoln looked up at the waiter with his brows furrowed.

"Ms. Barnett paid one hundred and fifty dollars

toward dinner and drinks for you," Kevin said as he handed Lincoln a folded note and leather-bound menu.

He read it but, in his mind, he heard her sultry voice. "'Maybe a meal and drinks will change your mood for the better. Find your inner peace. B,'" he mouthed before tossing the note atop the table.

Lincoln glanced back over his shoulder again. Bobbie was gone and the angry wife was now sitting across from her philandering husband in the booth, effectively blocking the mistress from exiting their heated exchange. Their voices weren't raised but the intensity was clear.

And so was the fear and shock of the mistress.

Cheating was not worth the hassle.

It had never been in his character to lie to one woman while wooing another one. He was always clear to anyone he invited in his life just where he stood. Whether only dating or a no-strings fling. Thus, the recent end of his latest entanglement. After a few months with Raven, her desire for strings had led to far too many heated arguments and chilly moments.

"Mr. Cress?" Kevin nudged.

Lincoln quickly perused the menu of high-end American cuisine. "The brioche shrimp toast to start. Roasted chicken with arugula next and then cheesecake to finish," he said, before snapping the menu closed.

"And your drink?" he asked, tucking the menu under his arm.

"Scotch. Neat," Lincoln said as he withdrew his phone from the inside pocket of his tailored blazer. His shoulders tensed at the series of twelve missed texts from his mother. Poppy Bridges was upset with him. Pissed, really. He stopped answering the endless calls to berate him for being a traitor and then the texts began. He had put his phone on Silent to avoid the constant vibrating.

Lincoln adored his mother—even if she was a handful.

Poppy loved good music, a good laugh and a good time. As a barmaid, she had enjoyed all three nearly nightly, leaving Lincoln to feel more like the parent than the child. They lived in the small flat above the pub and it had been routine for him to get himself off to school every morning as she slept after her shift ended when the bar closed at one in the morning. There had been little structure, barely any rules and lots of tirades about Phil Cress knocking her up and running away to Paris without a care for his kid.

Growing up, as a boy longing for a father, he had held out hope that it wasn't true. Adulthood had added lots of skepticism and a load of resentment.

As soon as his drink was set before him, Lincoln indulged in a deep sip. He had a lot to chew on besides Poppy's irrational fears of him abandoning her and his life in England to be with his father.

Phillip Cress Senior.

It was a desire to feel connected to his father—and a love of cooking—that led to Lincoln becoming a chef. He took pride in the achievement of his restaurant receiving a Michelin star awarded by the world-renowned travel guide in publication since the 1900s. His success was not by association with the successful culinary family.

Phillip Cress Senior and his wife, Nicolette Lavoie-Cress, had turned their over-five-decades careers as acclaimed and well-respected chefs into Cress, INC., a culinary empire with restaurants, nationally syndicated cooking shows, cookware, online magazines, an accredited cooking school and a nonprofit foundation. Each of their five sons, also successful chefs, worked for the empire they would one day inherit.

And now, at forty-four, with his own life firmly established, Lincoln was thrust into their lives and feeling like the outsider he was.

The bastard child.

DNA tests confirmed he was indeed Phillip's bastard son and Lincoln's inclusion in his will made him an illegitimate heir.

Not exactly the move of a man who would shirk his duties as a father.

Lincoln set aside his phone and thoughts on the Cress family—*his* family—as he enjoyed his meal. He longed for a bit more garlic on the roasted potatoes but enjoyed them along with the well-seasoned meat.

"I hate to see a gorgeous man eat alone."

With his fork paused before his open mouth, Lincoln cut his eyes up to find a tall, svelte redhead in a formfitting white dress and a seductive smile that was an invitation for more. A bit too forward for his taste. He frowned with annoyance. Deeply.

"And I hate that you assumed I would want to change that," he said tersely before sliding his fork into his mouth.

"Ooh. How rude," the woman said, clearly insulted.

"And interrupting my dinner wasn't?" he balked.

Lincoln was glad when she retreated and returned to her table where three other women awaited her. Within moments of her obviously filling them in on their exchange, all four women shot him glares that he ignored.

He was in America to gauge if he wanted or needed a relationship with his father. Finding love—or a sexy one-night stand—was not a part of the plan.

Tired of the continued scowls and done with his meal, Lincoln signaled for the waiter to bring the bill. Once it was in his hand, he snarked at Bobbie's hundred-fifty-dollar contribution. To counter it he left the waiter a hundred-dollar tip. "Also, Kevin, send the ladies at that table a bottle of champagne with my apologies," he said as he rose, acknowledging his abruptness and short patience was off-putting.

He was stern and no-nonsense. For many that was formidable. He just never had time for frivolities.

Once in the back of one of the Cress family's vehicles that had been assigned to him, Lincoln looked out the rear of the tinted window at the bright lights and fast movement of Midtown Manhattan. It was such a contrast from his hometown of St. Ives. There were sandy beaches and not towering high-rises of glass and metal. A slower pace. Small community. Familiarity and warmth.

Lincoln had only left St. Ives once before to attend culinary school in Switzerland. Upon its completion, he headed back home to work his way up in restaurants from prep cook to executive chef. And after more than a decade he struck out on his own, purchasing the pub where his mother had worked to convert it to his restaurant, SHORES.

This was his first trip to the states—to the hustle and bustle of New York City of all places.

He was *adjusting.*

The SUV rolled to a stop in front of the Cress family's five-story townhouse in the prominent and historic

Lenox Hill section of Manhattan's Upper East Side. The Victorian architecture of the ten-thousand-square-foot home was impressive. And the interior was just as daunting with staff quarters, wine cellar, chef's kitchen, elevator and movie room with six-bedroom suites and the entire third floor dedicated as the owner's quarters.

Lincoln stood on the sidewalk of the pristine neighborhood. He was a man of means, but nothing near that of his father and stepmother. With their wealth, he wondered just how much his presence was truly welcomed.

In the words of Lauryn Hill: "It's funny how money change a situation."

And do they think it's my motivation, because it's not.

Lincoln opened the gate of the wrought iron fence lining the front of the property. He jogged up the stairs but paused in using the key he was given. A surprising move when he was a stranger to them.

Not a total stranger after Bobbie Barnett searched my life with the accuracy of a colonoscopy scope.

He frowned.

Glad to see the last of her.

The wrought iron door opened and Lincoln gave a nod of greeting to Felice, the middle-aged housekeeper in a gray uniform. "Good evening, Mr. Cress," she said stepping back to allow him to move past her into the marble vestibule. "Did you lose your key?"

"No."

This is not my home.

Felice gave him a hesitant smile before moving past him in the entry to open the door leading directly into the home. The high tray ceilings with brocade design were reminiscent of the home's original Victorian era. Modern furnishings of gray and steel blue throughout the entire townhouse were luxurious and stylish. It was almost like it was staged for a spread in a glossy architectural magazine.

"Everyone is in the dining room," Felice said.

"I've already eaten so I'll just go up to my room," he said, already edging past her to the wrought iron staircase running along the north side of the home. "If you'll make my apologies."

"Yes. I will. You have a good night."

He paused on the steps to look back at her and was surprised by the compassion in her eyes. Or was it pity? With a stiff nod, Lincoln turned and continued up the stairs.

Two

"Ohm. Ohm. Ohm," Bobbie repeated as she sat nude atop a yellow yoga mat, her hair piled atop her head, and in a cross-legged Burmese position. Relaxing music played from an app on her tablet as she meditated and centered her thoughts on peace, happiness and balance.

She was all about positive energy and spiritual awakening—most times she succeeded.

Meditation, numerology, believing in angel/spirit guides and cleansing her home with sage to find inner peace were a part of her wheelhouse since the end of her marriage. She had needed something to believe in when she felt so lost and hurt from his affair.

Bzzzzzz.

"Ohm. Ohm. Ohm," Bobbie repeated, not wanting her peace disturbed by the vibrating of her phone.

Bzzzzzz.

"Damn it," she swore, opening one eye to glare at her cell phone across her loft atop the island in the kitchen area.

Bzzzzzz.

Everyone in her life knew that the early mornings were about her daily rituals of meditating and drinking tea as she journaled.

Only one person would ignore that.

Releasing a heavy breath Bobbie leaned to the left to answer the call on her iPad and abruptly bring the music to an end. "Good morning, Pops," she said, rising to pull on her robe before she looked up at the colorful sunrise displayed through the glass roof across the entire two thousand square feet of her loft.

Whether looking up at sunrises and sunsets, basking in the rays of the sun, daydreaming while looking up at the clouds or getting lost in the moon and the stars at night—the roof was the reason she purchased the space. That and the convenience of it being above the offices of B. Barnett Investigations.

"Busy?" Bobby Barnett asked, his voice gruff from years of smoking and yelling—whether called for or not.

"You *know* that I was, Pops," she said.

He chuckled. "I forgot this is your time to do your hocus-pocus stuff," he teased.

"No, you didn't," she said, moving from her yoga studio across the wide-planked hardwood floors of the converted two-story warehouse to the chef's kitchen. "And it's not magic. Try harder to be funny, Kevin Hardly."

Bobby laughed at her ribbing.

Bobbie smiled as she moved about the kitchen preparing a cup of oolong tea. The sunlight glinted off the copper appliances, butcher-block countertops and bronzed glazed wooden cabinets.

"And since you won't respect my morning customs of trying to heal my broken pieces, Pops, I'll just put my phone on Do Not Disturb until I'm done," she said, picking up the remote to open the cream flax linen drapes covering the windows lining the front of the loft.

"Yeah right," her father said with another chortle.

It was Bobby Barnett, detective extraordinaire, who had raised her when her mother, Haven, passed away from a heart attack when Bobbie was just eight years old. Her gruff but lovable father had been strict but quick to explain his duty to raise her to be a good person.

Bobbie adored him and would deny him nothing. And he knew it.

"How's the Atlantic Ocean?" she asked as she left her tea to steep.

"Perfection," he stressed with joy. "Plenty of Florida sun. Plenty of fish. And a beautiful woman to share it with makes me a happy man."

Bobbie rolled her eyes. "TMI, Pops," she drawled.

"How's the business?" he asked.

She walked over to the section of the counter she used as a work area. After opening her encrypted laptop, she eyed the surveillance photos she recently took. "Busy," she replied, thinking of the three cases she was currently juggling: a round of deep-dive background checks for a tech firm's new hires, investigating missing inventory at a computer factory and shadowing yet another cheating spouse.

On top of that, Bobbie monitored a large staff of investigators.

"You need me back?" Bobby asked, after a long pause.

"No. Enjoy your retirement," she assured him. "The team and I have it, Pops. I promise."

Bobbie inherited B. Barnett Investigations from her father just over a year ago. The former accomplished police detective had left the force to form his private investigation firm. After thirty years as a PI on call nearly 24/7, Bobby had decided it was time to enjoy his own life and pass the business on to his daughter who worked for him. He spent his free time cruising, deep-sea fishing and enjoying time with a woman friend depending on where he docked for the night.

"And?"

Bobbie strained her tea of the loose leaves and took a deep satisfying sip. "And what, Pops?" she asked with a little smack of her lips.

"Are you dating? All work and no play, kiddo," he advised her.

"Not even thinking about that for ten more months, Pops. Maybe more," she reminded him.

He sighed. "You're giving Henny too much power."

An image of her husband in bed with another woman flashed.

Bobbie flinched and pressed her eyes shut as she gripped the cup tighter. Pain radiated across her chest. Actual heartbreak. After their bitter divorce was finalized two months ago, she promised herself a full year—or more—before dating again.

To heal.

To recover.

To grow.

To learn the lesson.

"The last thing I need is to take my emotional bag-

gage into a new relationship," she said, hearing the softness in her voice caused by sadness.

"But, Bobbie—"

"Please, Daddy," she stressed, reverting to her childhood name for him.

"I love you, baby girl."

She opened her eyes and was comforted by the sun's
rays beaming onto the loft and its furnishings. A tear
raced down her cheek and she hung her head causing
her hair to fall forward and frame her face. "I know,"
she admitted.

"Hey! Hey! Hey!" Bobby said enthusiastic and loud
as ever. "Go back to doing that thing like Tina Turner
in 'What's Love Got to Do with It.'"

That caused her to chuckle. Her father would call
meditation anything but what it was. "Meditation," she
informed him for the hundredth time.

He grunted. "Right. *That.*"

"Got to go, Pops," she said, moving out of the kitchen
and over to the living room space decorated in rose gold
and cream with bronze accents.

"I'll call you later tonight," he said before ending
the call.

Bobbie freed her wild mane and dropped down onto
one of the four love seats positioned in a square around
the low-slung coffee table topped with copper pennies
under tinted glass. The idea of love and marriage used
to be so simple before that day she followed her husband
to that hotel. Her father balked at the year she promised herself, but as pain gripped her chest she wondered
if even that would be enough to heal her heart before
opening it to love once again.

* * *

Lincoln had a long stretch atop the king-size bed of his suite at the town house before rising to sit on the side of the bed naked. Still wiping sleep from his eyes as he yawned, he rose and made his way across the wooden floors of the wide bedroom to the en suite to relieve himself. His morning erection led the way. He took a few minutes to brush his teeth and wash his face before going back into the suite decorated in shades of gray, from charcoal to smoke.

He grabbed his phone from the nightstand as he reclaimed his seat atop the gray coverlet and crisp white cotton sheets on the bed. With an audible breath, he opened his online banking app. Between his business and personal accounts there had been six figures. With the transfer from Phillip Cress the amount had swelled to eight figures. He was far from destitute with his beachside home, a couple of cars, stocks and ownership of his thriving restaurant, but there was a wide gap between comfortable to massive abundance.

Lincoln hadn't wanted the money. Phillip Senior insisted he took it.

The thing he wanted most was the truth and that was free.

Was this massive windfall from his father about assisting the son he never knew about or to appease his guilt for never stepping up for the child he ignored?

Who is the liar?

The mother who raised him or the father he never knew?

It's time. No need to avoid it any longer.

Lincoln reached to grab his black pajama bottoms from where he had laid them atop the folded blanket across the foot of the bed—in case of an emergency overnight to quickly cover his nudity. After snatching them on and adjusting the elastic waist to fit below his abs, he grabbed his phone and walked over to open the gray suede curtains. The entire rear wall of the Cress townhome was glass and he looked out at emerald leaves of the towering tree in the backyard. In the distance, the sun glistened brightly above the city landscape.

It was seven thirty in the morning in New York, making it twelve thirty in the afternoon in England.

He FaceTimed his mother. As she answered, Lincoln steeled himself because with Poppy *anything* was possible. Her face filled the screen. She was a pretty silver-haired woman with hints of blond from her youth. Her long false lashes and red lipstick were in place as always.

Very similar to Nicolette.

Phillip Senior has a type.

"Ay! Well look who *finally* remembered his old mum, mates," Poppy said, turning the phone around to show her bevy of friends at the Pheasant & Pints Pub.

Lincoln frowned as they all began to greet him with raucous energy and lifts of their pints of beer. He had no doubt his mother was covering a round or two for all there. He would of course pay the bill upon its arrival to him.

"He's in a bad mood as ever, love," someone in the crowd shouted with a thick Cornish accent, bringing on laughs.

Releasing a heavy breath that only hinted at his frustration, Lincoln ended the FaceTime and then called her back via a phone instead.

"Okay, okay, Linc. Get your knickers out a twist, son," Poppy said as soon as she answered.

"And take me off Speaker," he ordered calmly.

She sighed.

Suddenly the background noise lessened.

"You've been wearing out my battery with calls and texts so I assumed you wanted to talk to me, not have a group chat," he said, again feeling more like the parent in their relationship.

"How's the wanker?"

Lincoln massaged his brow with a shake of his head at her insult of Phillip being a contemptible person. "Proclaiming he never knew you were pregnant," he said as he shifted his eyes down to the beautifully arched framework of bamboo leaves that covered the full thirty-two-foot length of the wall of his bedroom.

"Bloody twit," she snapped.

"Mum," Lincoln admonished her for calling his father silly.

"Don't you be a proper muppet," she warned.

"I'm no one's fool."

Poppy snorted in derision.

"Mum," Lincoln said again.

The line went quiet.

He worked his shoulders to relieve them of the building tension.

"Say you believe me, Linc," she said, her voice weepy and barely a whisper.

And there it is. Right on cue. The Poppy stunt.

Since he was a kid, whenever she broke a promise or did something that embarrassed him in public, she would give him a teary look, quivering lips and soft voice filled with "woe is me."

"What exactly happened between you two?" he asked, pressing on beyond her maneuver to distract him. "Outside of calling him everything from dishonest to the left teste of a circus clown, you have never explained what went down."

"Say you *believe* me, Linc," she repeated.

Lincoln whirled and tossed his phone in complete exasperation. Thankfully it landed on the middle of the bed.

Poppy Bridges was an eternal child. Even in her sixties.

She was the reason he found little humor in things and was so serious. Fun and frivolity had never been his choice. He was hell-bent not to be like his mother. He loved her—adored and spoiled her—but her carefree way of life was maddening to him and the order he preferred.

"Say you believe *me*, Linc," she repeated, her voice barely above a hoarse whisper.

He eyed the bed. It seemed her voice came from beneath the covers. It would be comical if he was ever up for a laugh. Lincoln threw up both hands. "Goodbye, Mum," he said, crossing the room to snatch up the phone and end the call.

She instantly called back.

He turned off the ringer and tossed it back onto the bed with a hard flick of his wrist. "Bloody hell," he snapped as he jumped in place ten times and shook his hands before rotating his neck. If he was home, he would have had a swift run on the beach. Instead, he dropped to the gray area rug for push-ups with his fists pressed to the floor.

He lost count but began to feel strain in the muscles of his arms. He kept going. The exercise was his relief—especially for his biggest headache. His mom.

Knock-knock.

Pausing with his arms straightened, he looked over at the pale gray wooden door.

He rose with ease and grabbed the top of the pajamas: not quite sure the door wouldn't burst open with the entire household—housekeeper and chef included. As he crossed the room, he eased the garment over his sweat-soaked arms and chest. He waited until he was fully buttoned up before opening the door.

"Good morning, Phillip Senior," Lincoln said eyeing his father, a tall and solid dark-skinned man with broad features, already fully dressed in a custom-made three-piece suit with a stylish silk paisley tie.

Just like a proper British gentleman.

Like him, Phillip was from St. Ives. He'd made quite a success of his life after leaving it at eighteen to attend culinary school in Paris. His successes were well-known back home and many were proud and boastful of him—except Poppy. Even with her constant scorn, secretly he also had been proud of the man.

Am I a muppet?

"Did I wake you?" Phillip asked with his British accent still prominent. He stepped inside the bedroom site. "The family's already downstairs for breakfast. Chef prepared brioche French toast and homemade chicken sausage. If that's not to your liking you can request whatever you like."

Lincoln fought not to frown at the expectation for all meals to be eaten together. It was so formal. So different from his solitary lifestyle. Most days he ate at the restaurant. Even growing up he had eaten alone while his mother worked. He couldn't imagine still living with his mother. Except for Cole and Gabe, his half brothers lived in the town house including Phillip Junior, his wife and five-year-old daughter. And here he was now living amongst them as well.

It's only for two weeks and then I'm going home.

"Sure, I'll be right down," Lincoln said.

Phillip Senior gave him a stiff smile. The air between them was still so awkward. They weren't much more than the strangers they were a few days ago. And in that short time, Lincoln had observed him as a stern man with a formidable presence.

Much like himself.

His father nodded as he turned to open the door. He paused in the entry. "I haven't asked about Poppy," he said with his eyes cast on the floor of the family den located in the center of the fourth floor flanked by three suites on one side and the elevator, wrought iron stairs and pantry on the other—identical to the fifth floor.

Lincoln wondered just what Phillip was thinking of the young woman he hadn't seen since they were eighteen. "She's well," he said, protecting her and his childhood with her.

Like always.

Phillip nodded solemnly with his mouth turned downward. "Perhaps she and I should talk," he said.

"Bloody twit."

As his mother's insult replayed in his head, Lincoln only said, "Perhaps."

Phillip Senior gave him one last sharp nod and closed the door as he left.

Shaking his head at the hell the man was contemplating provoking, Lincoln removed his pajamas and made his way to the bathroom for a quick shower.

Twenty minutes later he emerged from the suite in a dark blue linen blazer with a matching polo shirt and crisp denims with handmade shoes in caramel with denim blue trim. He checked his watch as he passed the light gray velvet sectionals and crossed the silk Persian carpet in shades of gray and steel blue to reach the stairs. His sous chef, Zander, was ordered to call him daily in between the lunch and dinner service for an update on SHORES.

Good. There's time.

He took the three flights of stairs, quickly landing in the living room and then making the right to eventually pass the kitchen on his left and the elevator on his right before entering the dining room at the rear of the house. The backyard was framed by the glass wall behind the long dining room table topped with charcoal leather and surrounded by armless suede chairs that were occupied.

"Good morning," he greeted everyone as he moved around the table.

Raquel, the wife of Phillip Junior, and their daughter, Collette, were already rising from their seats. "Hello, Lincoln. It's time to get this little one to day school," she said, before bending to press kisses to her husband's mouth as the five-year-old ran around the entire table and bestowed kisses to the cheeks of her grandparents at the opposing ends of the table, her uncles Sean and Lucas, and her father.

She ran over to Lincoln with a huge smile and bright eyes that couldn't be dimmed by the pink frame of her spectacles. *"Mon grand-père dit que tu es mon nouvel oncle,"* she said in fluent French.

"In English," Nicolette said, her own French accent very pronounced.

"My grandfather says you are my new uncle," Collette interpreted.

Lincoln cast the regal woman in her sixties a brief look before looking down at his adorable niece again. *"Je parle un peu Français. Et oui, je suppose que je suis votre Oncle Lincoln,"* he said, explaining that he did speak a little French and that he was indeed her uncle.

Colli's smile broadened before she flung her arms open wide and then clamped them around his legs in a tight hug.

Lincoln stiffened in surprise until she released him.

"Au revoir, Oncle Lincoln," she said excitedly before taking off at a run.

Everyone around the table chuckled as Lincoln cleared his throat and claimed the seat Raquel vacated to Nicolette's right, leaving a space between himself and Phillip Junior. His half brother looked less than pleased at his daughter's declaration.

I'm sick of him.

A short and plump man in a red chef's coat walked over to him. "What would you like for breakfast?" he asked.

Lincoln barely looked at the printed menu atop his place setting. "Just coffee. My first meal is usually lunch," he explained. "But thank you."

"Yes, thank you, Chef Carlisle," Nicolette said with a formal smile.

Lincoln was still trying to figure everyone out, but from the few times he had been in the presence of the culinary queen he felt there was more to her than what she chose to show. It made it difficult to trust her.

"Lincoln, the family eats together as often as we can," she said, with a smile that barely reached her eyes.

Lincoln took a sip of the brew. It was delicious. A custom blend. Strong and nutty.

"We missed you at dinner," Nicolette added.

"I had dinner out," he offered, feeling as if he was being reprimanded and not liking it.

"Alone?" she asked.

He locked eyes with her blue ones—they assessed him. Perhaps she didn't trust him either.

"Nicolette," Phillip Senior interjected firmly.

She smiled before wiping the corners of her mouth with her linen napkin.

Phillip Senior set his utensils down on his plate. "Lincoln, I don't know if you're familiar with Cress, INC.—"

"I am," Lincoln admitted.

"Of course, he is," Phillip Junior muttered.

Really sick of him.

Sean and Lucas shared a look before shooting Phillip Junior a hard stare.

Maybe I'm not the only one.

"Each of my sons holds an executive position at the company. Gabe heads up the restaurant division and runs his restaurant. Phillip Junior oversees The Cress Family Foundation. Sean supervises the syndicated cooking shows. Cole oversees digital marketing and global branding via our online magazines and websites. And our youngest, Lucas, is head of the cookware line," he explained. "Lincoln, we wanted to talk to you about a position at Cress, INC."

"What!" Phillip Junior exclaimed as he snatched his napkin off his lap and slammed it atop his plate.

"Man, chill out and get over it, Phil," Sean snapped, his voice filled with his irritation.

"It's enough, man. For real," Lucas agreed, shoving his plate of fresh fruit away in frustration.

Phillip Junior jumped to his feet. "You're going to sit here and say nothing while the five of us have been at each other's throats for the CEO position when Dad retires and now, he's just throwing another damn hat in the ring!" he exclaimed.

And enough is enough.

"You know, Phillip, I'm sorry the biggest thing you had going for you was being the heir apparent firstborn son—or at least *thought* you were," Lincoln said with a coldness toward his half brother that had been stewing with every insult thrown his way by him.

"Go to hell!" Phillip roared.

Lincoln nodded with coolness. "Let's see if I got it right," he said. "Sean's the star. Right?" he asked, jerking his thumb in the direction of the brother who favored Daniel Sunjata.

"True," Sean agreed with a one-shoulder shrug unable to deny his appeal as the host of several shows and attendee of celebrity A-list parties on the regular.

"Gabriel's the good one and Cole is the rebel so he could care less about it," Lincoln continued. "And Lucas is the favorite. Did I get it right?"

Lucas, the youngest Cress son, dared to look bashful at the truth just spoken.

"Who the hell do you think *you* are?" Phillip Junior said.

"The eldest Cress brother," Lincoln said with a simplicity that was mocking.

Phillip Junior took a step in Lincoln's direction prompting him to calmly rise to his feet.

"Assez!" Nicolette snapped with a sharp clap of her hands, letting them know it was enough.

Phillip Junior stopped his forward motion and walked away from Lincoln to pace.

Lincoln released a heavy breath as he reclaimed his seat. He wasn't quite sure this whole scenario wouldn't play out like the script of an ITV mystery where one brother killed another to avoid sharing a hefty inheritance.

Phillip Junior better not try me. I would snap him in half.

Like a dried twig.

"I think it's very clear that Lincoln must spend time with all of his brothers and forge a relationship with them. War is not an option," Nicolette said.

"And anyone hoping to one day become CEO of a company built for the family by the family should feel the same," Phillip Senior finally spoke up. "Lincoln is family now. And he deserves the same opportunity to step into my shoes as *any* of my sons."

"Listen," Lincoln began. "I appreciate how welcoming most of you have been. But I have a life back in England. My mother. My restaurant. I need to—and will—return home in two weeks."

Phillip Senior looked grim while his namesake could barely contain his pleasure at Lincoln's announcement.

Bobbie freed her hair from its topknot as soon as she climbed behind the wheel of her blacked-out electric SUV parked in the underground garage in Manhattan's Upper East Side. She wove her fingers through the strands and shook them loose as she massaged her scalp, glad to have it unrestrained once again. The hair and the black gabardine evening dress she wore were for undercover surveillance at a charity gala at The Metropolitan Museum of Art. As soon as she got home, the laced stilettos would go next.

She opened her laptop sitting on the mount attached to the passenger seat bolt and logged into her encrypted account. Her fingers flew as she updated the file on the tech CEO suspected of selling intel to the company's competitors. She was uploading surveillance photos from her sequined clutch that was a camera in disguise.

She paused to cover her mouth with the back of her hand as she yawned.

Private investigative work was exhausting at times, but she loved it. Even as she had stepped into the role of the owner upon her father's retirement, she had not lessened her workload. Instead, she relied heavily on her team for needed support.

And the work she did was good.

No matter what anyone *thinks.*

Especially him.

Lincoln Cress.

Her fingers paused as his words of scorn echoed.

Find another occupation where you're not paid to lie, pretend and exploit people who did not choose to have you in their lives...

"Bully," she muttered, resuming her typing.

What a waste of a sexy man.

Bobbie paused again with her fingers floating above the keyboard at the surprising thought. He was handsome. And fit. And attractive. She arched a brow and pressed her hand to her throat. Her pulse pounded a bit harder than before.

Bzzzzzz.

She looked down at her phone sitting in the lap of her voluminous skirt. She gasped to see THE BRUTE calling. Lincoln. That's how she'd saved his number in her contacts as she left the restaurant last night. It was unnerving for him to call just as she thought of him. With her heart pounding, she answered the call and placed it on Speaker.

"B. Barnett," she said crisply.

"This is Lincoln. Lincoln Cress."

His voice was deep and his British accent made it intriguing.

"I need to hire you," he continued.

Bobbie chuckled sarcastically. "*Nooooooo.* Not *me*," she said in a singsong fashion. "Not my exploitive work that you disdain, Mr. Cress."

He released a breath that echoed throughout the car. "Have your moment," he said stiffly.

"Gladly," she smirked as she sat back against the red leather driver's seat and tapped her nails against the steering wheel. "I *told* you to be careful that you might need my services."

Lincoln remained quiet.

"Isn't this something?"

"Are you done?" he drawled.

Bobbie inhaled sharply and released an exhale with a moan. "*Am* I?" she asked.

"Listen, can we meet? Tonight," he said.

"It's pretty late, Mr. Cress," she said, eyeing the time on the dash of her vehicle.

"It's urgent," Lincoln stressed.

Curiosity was her downfall. Always was. Always would be.

"Can you meet me in front of The Met on Fifth Avenue?" she asked, already closing her laptop and easing the mount down until it was under the passenger seat.

"On the way," he said, before ending the call.

"Rude," Bobbie muttered as she opened the glove compartment and removed her high-voltage Taser to slide inside her camera clutch.

Just in case.

She left her car and locked it with the key fob before taking long strides across the garage to ride the elevator up to the street. The sounds of New York were activated and loud as ever. The blare of car horns. The grind of motors of vehicles. The laughs, shouts and other noises of those revving up for nightlife. The blare of music from cars and businesses.

New York.

She loved the pulse and the energy.

"Sweet God! Marry me!" someone shouted with a thick Italian accent as a car whizzed past her.

Bobbie just smiled and continued her stride.

As she paused at the corner of East Eighty-Fourth Street and Fifth Avenue she eyed the towering structure with French Beaux-Arts architecture now in existence for over a century and a half. The steps of one of the country's largest museums of art were regal and beautiful, particularly at night with the illumination.

Bobbie crossed the walkway once the light permitted.

People still loitered on the many steps leading up to the main entrance of The Met. Some were jean-clad tourists and others like herself were there for the event and dressed as such. As she came to a stop in front of the building, she pulled her ostrich feather shawl closer around her shoulders because of the crisp winter air.

"Ms. Barnett."

Bobbie turned at Lincoln weaving amongst the pedestrians on the street to reach her. He wore a camel overcoat that looked to be quality cashmere. She didn't miss that several women looked him over as he moved past them with long strides.

He's bowlegged.

As he came to a stop before her, his eyes gave her a hard assessing up-and-down look. "That's quite a getup," he said.

"I was undercover," she explained, fighting her annoyance with him.

His mouth was always his downfall.

"As what?" he asked.

She imagined how she looked to him. Her dress had a full A-line skirt that rested above her knees and the thin straps of the bodice came down to a deep vee to the strap around her waist, pushing her cleavage forward daringly. Her makeup was more dramatic than when he last saw her with a smoky eye, blush and her gloss now a shimmery pale pink.

"Have you nothing nice to say? *Ever?*" she asked in exasperation.

Lincoln looked surprised. "What did I say that wasn't nice?" he asked.

She widened her eyes and looked down at the tips of his tailored shoes as she allowed herself a five-count—before she whipped out her Taser. A gust of chilly wind blew and she felt her hair raise from her shoulders, and back from her face. She looked up at him.

Lincoln looked startled.

She turned to see what caused the expression. "Something wrong?" she asked, glancing back at him.

His handsome face was back to its normal sternness. "No," he said.

Whatever.

"How can I help you, Mr. Cress?" she asked, ready to be free of him.

"I need you to pretend to be my girlfriend while I'm in New York," he said without hesitation.

"Say what?" Bobbie asked, knowing her face was a mask of confusion.

"Look. The Cress family is a bit much for my taste. It's all too much. And they want me to take part in a bunch of family events while I'm here," he said brusquely.

She knew from her investigation that Lincoln was an only child of an only child and there was no other family. She could understand how a large bunch like the Cress family could take getting used to.

Especially for this guy, she thought, considering his perpetual bad mood.

"Why me?" she asked him.

"You're the only other person I know in the country," he said.

"No girlfriend?" she asked, shifting to the left a bit to avoid a group of women laughing and walking in her direction.

"Here?" he asked as if she was foolish.

"Anywhere," she countered.

He shook his head. "No. Definitely not."

Surprise. Surprise.

"By *choice*," he added as if instantly thinking back to her assertion that he needed great sex in his life.

She guessed there were idiotic, self-love-starved women in the world who went for the rough and rude type. She wasn't one of them. For work or play. "Mr. Cress, we don't mix and I think it's best we stick to staying out of each other's lives because—"

"Isn't this the type of thing you do as PI? Pretend?" he asked, his eyes searching her face.

She shook her head. "Uhm. No. Not for this type of scenario—"

"Fifty thousand," he said, his tone clipped.

"Dollars?" Bobbie shrieked.

"No, buttons," Lincoln said with sarcasm. "Of course, dollars."

Bobbie wasn't lacking money at all, but fifty grand was nothing to balk at. She studied him. Was it worth risking an assault charge to use self-defense moves to strangle him until his sarcastic tongue rolled out of his mouth?

He checked the time on his watch before sliding his hands into the pockets of his overcoat.

"Is it that bad?" she asked, her soft tone surprising her.

And from the look on his face, him as well. "Yes," he admitted with obvious reluctance.

And that did it. Bobbie always rooted, cheered and helped the underdog.

Even one who was a tool.

"Okay," she agreed, instantly feeling she would regret it.

He nodded. "The first get-together is tomorrow," he said.

"Thus, the urgency tonight," she assumed.

"Right."

"Let's meet up beforehand to get our story straight," she recommended.

"I'll call you in the morning," he said, before turning and striding away.

Am I really doing this?

She stood there on the steps of The Met and watched his tall figure until he disappeared amongst the crowd.

Three

Lincoln climbed from the back of the chauffeured SUV. He stood on the street looking up at the two-story brick warehouse as the sun slowly began to set. The bronzed placard on the building read B. BARNETT INVESTIGATIONS. Established 1981. He looked up and down the street in what he discovered to be the Tribeca section of Manhattan.

It was more than he expected, particularly since Bobbie had always met him outside an office up until that day and there was nothing about her that implied an affiliation with corporate America. Nothing.

Her hair was constantly the epitome of windblown.

As he opened the tinted glass door, he paused at the image of her hair splayed atop a bed as she arched her back in passion. Clearing his throat at the impropriety of his thoughts, he entered. To his right was a glass-enclosed waiting room with leather club chairs and a wall-mounted flat-screen television. Twenty glass cubicles lined both sides of the exposed brick walls of the more than two-thousand-square-foot warehouse. A dozen or more people occupied the offices. Up the middle of the space a long wooden conference table that could seat twenty people was lined with lily floral arrangements in bronze vases. And at the other end of the table, against the far wall, was a glass-enclosed office with Bobbie sitting behind her large desk on the phone.

"Welcome to B. Barnett's. May I help you?"

Lincoln looked to his left at a reception area where a woman in her sixties with freckles and a pink-tinted silver bob was looking over the rim of her thick black spectacles at him. He walked over to the desk. "Lincoln Cress. I have an appointment with Bobbie Barnett," he said.

The lady pierced him with her hazel eyes. "Good morning," she said pointedly.

Lincoln frowned as he looked down at her. "Excuse me?" he asked.

She lowered the stylus she was holding poised above a tablet where she appeared to be playing a game. "Good. Morning," she repeated. "I thought the British were the epitome of propriety? Good morning is a greeting used when you first interact with someone."

Lincoln's back stiffened. "Lessons on manners, as you sit at work with pink hair, game playing and incorrectly attempting at reraising a grown man here to do business?" he asked.

The woman's mouth fell open into an O and her eyes widened. "No, you didn't," she gasped.

"Yes, I bloody did," he assured her.

"Well, I refuse to announce you until I am greeted properly," she said, crossing her arms over her chest.

He waved his hand at her as if to shoo her. "Don't be absurd," he snapped.

She only leaned back in her conference chair, crossed her legs and arched a silver brow.

Lincoln returned her glare.

They stared at one another.

Lincoln leaned forward a bit with his eyes still locked on hers.

She did the same.

Oh, bloody hell!

"Good morning," he chewed out.

Her smile revealed her satisfaction. "Good morning," she said pleasantly before leaning forward to press a button on her office phone with their eyes still locked.

"Yes, Ms. Pott?" Bobbie said via intercom.

"Mr. Cress is here," the woman said.

Lincoln looked down the length of the warehouse to see Bobbie look up at him.

"I'll be right out."

He continued to eye her as she rose and came from around the desk. She looked stunning in a tailored bright pink pantsuit with peaked lapels and structured shoulders. The slim fit captured her wide hips. Her hair was pulled back into a sleek low bun exposing her ever-present large and slender gold hoop earrings. Her long strides in her gold heels seemed in slow motion—like on a catwalk.

"Ready?" she asked with a husky voice and polite smile.

"Are you?" he asked.

Her smile faded and her brown eyes sparkled with annoyance. "What?" she stressed.

"It's dinner, not a business meeting," Lincoln explained.

She forced a smile that did not reach her eyes. "You better be glad your transfer cleared this morning," she said through clenched teeth as she turned. "Follow me, Mr. Cress."

"Lincoln," he said, causing her to turn back around. "Huh?"

"Shouldn't you call me by my first name?" he asked.

Bobbie chuckled—it was rich. "There are many things I would like to call you," she said.

"Me too," Ms. Pott said dryly from behind them.

Lincoln gave the other woman one last glare over his shoulder before following Bobbie down the length of the conference table and to the door of her office where she pressed her thumb against a biometric lock to open it.

He was impressed—and fighting like crazy not to watch the back-and-forth sway of her bottom as she moved over to a large elevator against the rear of the side wall. Another press of a biometric lock and the chrome doors slid open. She stepped inside and turned.

"Come," she bid.

The simple request caused his heart to quicken its pace as he stepped on beside her and the doors closed.

"This is quite a setup," he admitted.

"Oh. Oh my. A compliment?" she said in mock surprise.

"There are not many opportunities to provide one," he lied, admitting to himself that he enjoyed trading barbs with her.

The elevator slid to a stop. "When I took over from

my father, I invested a good bit of company funds to purchase the building. My father had been leasing it for years and I thought it was a good investment," she explained as the doors opened, revealing a loft apartment with glass ceilings that was inviting and warm.

"Stay here," she said, turning a key in the panel that left the elevator doors open.

He looked on as she kicked off her shoes, taking four inches off her height, and picked up a tray from the bronze-and-glass table against the wall by the entry. She used a mini torch to ignite a bundle of light green leaves wrapped into a roll with white thread. Smoke began to funnel up from it as the flame died out and the bundle smoldered.

She stepped back onto the elevator and began to wave the bundle up and down the length of his body.

He coughed from the acrid smell. "What is that?" he asked as she moved to circle him.

"Sage," she said from behind him. "You have a lot of negative energy and I don't want you shedding it in my home."

Lincoln released a breath heavy with his exasperation. "You can't be serious," he balked, turning to lightly grab her wrist and remove the sage from her hand. "The smell will get in my clothes…and my lungs."

Bobbie took it back from him and used the tray to snuff out the embers before setting it back down on the table. "Let me change. Have a seat," she said, before walking away.

Lincoln remained standing as he continued to look around her space. He was surprised she invited him inside it even though they were working together.

Even if she gave me a smoke shower.

He raised his arm to smell the sleeve of the maroon V-neck sweater he wore.

I smell like lit charcoals.

He paused when he noticed an area with rolled yoga mats, fat candles atop floor candleholders and a small bronze-topped table with an array of colorful crystals in various shapes and sizes, and another bundle of sage atop a tray.

So, she's deep into the spiritual thing.

He shook his head in judgment, holding no belief in actions akin to New Age mysticism.

Hocus-pocus bull.

Lincoln moved to the windows and looked down at the street where his vehicle and driver waited to chauffeur them to Gabe and Monica's. He slid his fingers into the front pockets of the dark denims he wore with espresso boots. The thought of the dinner with his brothers made his gut clench as the time drew near. He did not know them but they were his blood. His family. He was in New York to get to know them. To see if he fit into their world and whether he *wanted* them to fit into his.

He looked at the beautiful landscape of the setting sun over a bridge in the distance. The colors were vibrant as the day slowly shifted to the dark of night. For a moment he thought of the sunsets over the waters of St. Ives. It was his favorite time of the day. Even during hectic dinner service at the restaurant, he would find a moment to step out onto the deck used for elegant outdoor eating, sip from a glass of scotch and enjoy the view.

As the skies darkened, the windows of Bobbie's

apartment became transparent and suddenly, he could see her in a sheer fuchsia bra about to unzip her pants.

His heart thundered at the intoxicating sight of her. Even as he averted his eyes to respect her modesty, he was rushed with a hunger for more.

To see.

To touch.

To taste.

Just like last night.

As they stood before The Met and the night wind caught her hair, breezing it back from her face, Bobbie had looked up at him. She was stunning. The hair. Those lips. Her eyes. Just beautiful.

The urge to kiss her had filled him. Made him hungry.

And the dress. That dress.

As he walked toward her on the busy street, he had allowed himself to feast on the alluring sight of her. Bobbie personified sex appeal. And it appeared easily. Not forced. She was bold and confident and in full control of her being. And with a vibe that she also knew how to make a man feel like a man.

Great sex, she had said was one of the three things he needed in life.

He had no doubt she could provide that. Long into the night. Over and over—

"Lincoln?"

Startled by her husky voice, he jumped and cleared his throat at his heated thoughts. He turned to find her standing near the island in the kitchen in a black floral-embroidered open-knit sweater with a plunging V-neck partnered with crepe cargo pants that sat low on her curvy hips and exposed a bit of her belly. "How about this?" she said, striking mock fashion poses. "I assumed Mr. British would like the suit."

"I *really* like those pants on you," he admitted before he stopped the words.

His heart took off at a gallop. From desire and regret at what he revealed.

Bobbie's face filled with surprise as she came over to stand before him. "Why?" she asked with emphasis. Teasing him.

And tempting him without even trying.

Lincoln stiffened and stepped back from her. "It suits you better," he said, forcing formality into his tone.

She shrugged as she turned. "True," she agreed, walking back down the length of the loft to reach her bedroom where she opened a gold clutch to touch up her lip gloss.

Bobbie Barnett with her plump and glossy lips, wild hair and sexy Bohemian style were turning out to be more than Lincoln thought he could handle. Or ignore. Something about her—or maybe everything about her—drew him in. Tempted him. Made him curious about things.

Like, does she moan, whimper or cry out during sex?

Lincoln turned back to the window as he felt his desire stir and his entire body felt like he was coated in excitement.

Damn.

As he thought of the contentious feelings for one another, the challenge of charming and seducing her gave him a thrill but he knew he would not. He wasn't looking for a relationship of any kind. His time in New York was short. The circumstances surrounding his most recent breakup—a no-strings relationship that became very complicated—had him feeling averse to more flings.

Still...

He turned and locked his eyes on her as she pulled on a coat.

Sitting back and enjoying the provocative show that was Bobbie Barnett just being Bobbie Barnett was no trouble at all.

Right?

Bobbie entered her kitchen and picked up the remote to close the curtains—something she'd forgotten to do earlier in the day. "Ready?" she asked, setting the remote down and then tucking her clutch under her arm as she walked over to the elevator.

Lincoln gave her a stiff nod before coming down the length of the loft to reach her. She stepped on first. He followed.

"May I?" he asked.

She turned the key in the panel and the elevator's doors began to close, before looking over at him. "May you what?" she asked.

Lincoln placed his hands on her shoulders to gently turn her body to face his.

She arched a brow as she looked up at him. His intense eyes were on her face as he studied her. "What *now*?" she asked.

He reached up to remove the pins holding her mane back into a knot.

"Wow," she said, holding up her palm. "You don't like my hair either, huh?"

He set the pins in her hand as he removed them and then eased his fingers into the waves to shake them free until her hair was big and wild again. His fingers stroked her scalp. Bobbie released a soft gasp as a jolt of pure electricity coursed over her body. Like fire.

"I got it," she said, easing her head back to free her hair from his hands.

She turned away hoping he hadn't noticed her sudden rapid breaths and hard nipples pressing against her thin sweater. "I thought you would prefer it tamed," she said awkwardly, hoping to fill the silence with a joke.

"Definitely not," he said.

Bobbie's face filled with a curious look. It was a rare moment when she had nothing quick to retort with, but she was flustered. Her awareness of Lincoln and his revelation of liking her wild style had her shook up.

What in the world is going on?

Acknowledging that a man was handsome was entirely different from an attraction.

As the elevator descended and they made their way across the offices and out of the building, Bobbie waited for her awareness of him to subside. Like a fluke. But it remained. Like the low buzz in the background. Constant. Almost forgotten until it's not.

Bobbie paused as Lincoln waved away the driver from leaving his seat, to open the rear door of the SUV himself. When he turned and offered her his large hand, she eyed him as the streetlight shone right down upon his stern but handsome face, his height and broad shoulders. The maroon color looked good against his complexion and deepened the darkness of his eyes.

"Bobbie?" he said, eyeing her still standing there leaving his hand of assistance waiting.

She wanted to stroke his square jawline and soften his mouth with a smile.

And I could, she thought, picturing.

This dark, brooding man with the worst attitude she had encountered had stroked her scalp and now her belly was warm with desire.

She ignored his hand and brushed past him to climb onto the rear seat. As he entered the vehicle beside her and closed the door, the scent of his cologne seemed to strengthen. Bobbie shifted over to put more distance between them, nearly pressed to the door.

"I won't bite you, Ms. Barnett," Lincoln said.

I wouldn't mind.

She blinked to erase a vision of his head between her thighs as he nibbled his way up. "Bobbie," she said, swallowing over a lump in her throat. "Remember? First names."

"Right. Bobbie," he added.

She forced herself to relax as the chauffeur drove them away. "Which brother?" she asked.

"Coleman."

She thought of the man who favored Michael Ealy and their brother, Gabriel, who favored Jesse Williams. It was Cole and Gabe who hired her to investigate.

Does Lincoln know that?

"I'm sure you remember him and Gabe?" he drawled.

I guess he does.

Bobbie gazed at him. "It will be nice to see them out of a *professional* setting," she said.

Lincoln said nothing more as the ride continued to the Chelsea section of Manhattan's West Side where Cole resided with his fiancée, Jillian. Soon the vehicle pulled to a stop in front of a stately postwar building.

"Ready?" he asked, reaching for the door handle.

"Are you?" she shot back.

"You're right. I'm not a pro at pretending," he agreed.

"Says the man paying for my services," she retorted.

Lincoln had been about to exit but stopped to look back over his shoulder at her. "That doesn't sound the way you wanted it to," he advised her.

He's right.

"You know what I mean," she rushed to say.

Lincoln stepped out and offered his hand as Bobbie shifted across the leather seat. "Think you can bear to touch me this time or should I drop my hand now?"

Bobbie eased her hand into his as she stepped down out of the SUV. But only for a quick moment and with her fingertips barely touching his. They walked into the building as the doorman held the entry open for them.

"Are you sure you can stand being on the elevator with me?" he asked as they neared it.

"I don't know. Will there be enough room for me with all your arrogance?" she asked, stepping on and turning.

"With all that hair, I'm not sure," he balked, joining her.

The doors slid closed and the elevator rose.

"You seem fixated on my hair tonight," she said, reminding him—and herself—of his fingers grazing her scalp.

"Hardly," he drawled.

She turned to stand in front of him and poked his chest with her finger. It met firm resistance. Muscles and strength. "Do you work out?" she asked, completely distracted from her annoyance with him.

"You seem fixated on my body," Lincoln said, sounding smug.

Ding.

The elevator slid to a stop.

Bobbie looked up at him. "Hardly. You arrogant and rude ass—"

"Lincoln, you made it."

Bobbie turned to find the door open and Cole standing in the hall outside his apartment.

Cole looked surprised and then confused. "Ms. Barnett? Are you two...together?" he asked.

Bobbie blinked and went into work mode as she took Lincoln's hand in hers. "Yes, I guess we have to thank you and Gabe for bringing us together when you both hired me to find him," she said as they stepped off the elevator. She looked up at Lincoln with a warm smile. "We reconnected once he got into town and now we're enjoying each other's company again."

Lincoln nodded in agreement. "I couldn't wait to look her up and finish what we started," he said.

With warmth.

Bobbie was shocked but covered it well as she slid her arm around his as Cole led them into the apartment.

"Interesting plot twist," Cole said with a smile.

As Lincoln grabbed the lapels of her jacket to help remove her coat, his fingers grazed the sides of her neck. Bobbie shivered and quickly stepped away from his touch. Her steps faltered when everyone gathered in the living room looked in their direction.

A pretty woman with chin-length auburn curls in a winter white off-the-shoulder sweater and slacks walked over to greet them. "Welcome," she said with a warm smile as she took one of Bobbie's hands in both hers to squeeze. "I'm Jillian. Cole's fiancée."

"Bobbie. Bobbie Barnett," she said, feeling Lincoln fall in step at her side.

Jillian shifted to press a kiss on Lincoln's cheek. "And good to see you again, Lincoln," she said. "Come on in."

Lincoln placed a hand to the small of her back as she left the foyer and walked into the spacious living room that sported high ceilings and elegant navy decor with gold accents. Bobbie was so aware of his touch and confused by her reaction to it. Her body felt on high alert.

Am I that desperate for sex?

It had been five months since she left her cheating husband and filed for divorce. Surely though, even such a long time without intimacy would not make her vulnerable to a brute like Lincoln Cress.

She glanced up at his profile. Those high cheekbones and square jawline were undeniable.

He really is gorgeous.

Jillian made the introductions of everyone gathered, but truthfully, Bobbie recognized everyone but her from her investigations into Phillip Cress Senior. She refrained from saying that and patiently stood by, wishing she didn't know *things* about some of them—especially now that she was in their company.

Phillip Junior and his wife Raquel. Sean. Gabriel and Monica. And Lucas.

"Good to see you again, Bobbie," Monica said, walking over to hand both her and Lincoln flutes of champagne.

"Thanks. You too," she said, accepting the flute and taking a deep sip.

"Again?" Sean asked, looking up from his phone.

"Bobbie's the PI we hired to find Lincoln," Gabe said.

"What!" Phillip Junior exclaimed from his seat on the sofa.

"Let's sit down for dinner," Cole said, smiling as he used a finger to close Jillian's mouth which opened in shock. "Right, baby?"

"Uh—uh. Yeah. Yes. *Yes!* Let's eat," she said, recovering from her stammer. "Have a seat and we'll bring it all out."

Again, Lincoln's hand rested on her lower back as they all made their way to the dining room.

"Cut the crap, PJ, you know how to ruin a good time and I am getting sick of it."

Bobbie looked back over her shoulder at Raquel's harshly whispered words to her husband who looked every bit of an insolent pouting child. "What's that about?" she whispered to Lincoln.

"Him? Same crap on a different day" was all he said as he held her seat for her at the table before sitting beside her.

Bobbie looked on as Cole and Jillian began to carry in large porcelain platters. A family of skilled, award-winning chefs? *This should be good.*

"Okay," Cole said with a clap of his hands as he stood by the table. "What we have for you tonight is—"

"Come on now, fiancé. Tell 'em!" Jillian jokingly egged him on.

Cole chuckled as they eyed each other. "Tell 'em?" he asked.

"Tell *them*," she urged, doing a snake move in her chair and snapping her fingers.

They're adorable.

Bobbie looked around the table. Everyone was enjoying the couple's playfulness. Even Lincoln looked as amused as he could.

"Well tell us so we can eat. I'm hungry, bro," Sean

said, chuckling as he pushed up the sleeves of the powder-blue sweater he wore.

Laughter filled the air.

Bobbie was surprised. These were people of affluence who grew up in wealth and were surrounded by luxuries. She had heard and seen them before on television and in the press. She'd even eaten at both of their CRESS restaurants in New York. Never would she have imagined them so relatable and at ease.

She glanced over at Lincoln. He looked comfortable enough, but not as at ease as everyone else.

No wonder he feels out of place. Their camaraderie is deep and real.

"So, what we have is a seafood-centered menu for the night," Cole said. "There's oyster stew to start. Fried calamari and arugula salad with lemon vinaigrette. And then fried seafood pot pie with lobster, shrimp, lump crab and scallops."

"And for dessert, a baklava made with macadamia and walnuts," Jillian added, standing to take a quick bow. "You're welcome."

So, Jillian is a chef as well? Wow.

Cole took his seat at the end of the large glass table opposite his future bride. "Lincoln, we should have asked if you were allergic to seafood," he said, eyeing his eldest brother.

"He's not," Bobbie assured him as she took her turn ladling the delicious-smelling stew into her bowl.

Lincoln leaned in close to her.

Her pulse sped like crazy.

"You think you know everything about me," he whispered near her ear.

And that was her undoing.

She shivered and gasped. The closeness of him and the feel of his cool breath against her ear evoked thoughts of hot sex. Wild sex. Fast and furious. Then deep and slow.

The bud nestled by the lips of her intimacy pulsed with life.

Damn. We got a problem.

Bobbie set her unused spoon down and leaned over to grasp Lincoln's wrist for his attention. He bent his head down to her. "We have to talk," she said, not keeping the urgency from her voice.

Lincoln leaned back a bit to look down into her face. Their eyes met and held for countless moments before his fell to her mouth.

And then she knew.

He wants me too.

His eyes deepened in color and intensity. There was a surge of an unseen current between them.

Big problem.

"Just how did you two meet?" Phillip said, intruding on the electric moment.

His wife is right. He knows how to ruin a good time.

Bobbie broke their charged stare to eye Phillip directly across from them. She covered Lincoln's hand with her own and gripped it tight. "I went to London to research him. I was undercover but we both felt a strong attraction, but we didn't move on it," she said, glancing over at Lincoln.

"Just flirting a little bit," he said.

Just as they planned.

"Because I don't mix business and pleasure so nothing developed," she said, resetting her eyes on the man who favored the actor and former pro wrestler Dwayne "The Rock" Johnson. "Especially with me undercover."

Just as cute but not as charming. Not at all.

"But when I got to New York and asked for the name of the PI, I soon discovered the beautiful woman with the wild hair and the mouth that I couldn't stop thinking about," Lincoln added. "I forgot about confronting the PI for invading my life and was just happy to reconnect with her. And here we are. Right, baby?"

Bobbie looked over at him. His eyes were on her and she felt breathless.

Humongous problem.

She couldn't remember her part of the script. She couldn't think of much of anything except how delicious it would be to break her one-year rule to take a glorious ride atop one naked, sweaty and hard Lincoln Cress.

"Aww," the ladies all sighed in unison.

Awww hell.

Bobbie was glad when everyone resumed eating and Raquel glared at Phillip Junior for him to quell any further questioning of them. Again, she placed a hand on Lincoln's wrist atop the table to get his attention. And again, he bent his head down so that her ear was to his mouth.

Do my whispers excite him like his excited me?

She knew it might be rude to whisper, but so would excusing themselves to step away to talk. And it couldn't wait. She had to set things straight.

"I'm attracted to you, Lincoln," she began.

Her hand lightly rested against his inner wrist and she felt his pulse pound harder against her fingertips.

And that set her pulse off to the races as well, until she felt lightheaded.

"But I *can't* do anything about it because I'm recently divorced and promised myself a year of no dating and no sex. Nothing," she stressed.

Lincoln nodded in understanding before he shifted to place his mouth near her ear. "Same. I want you, Bobbie. Bad," he said, his voice deep and low.

She crossed her legs and released a heavy breath, fighting not to fan away the heat she felt rising.

"I'm in town for two weeks and it would be nothing more than a fling," he admitted.

She leaned back to lock eyes with him. His eyes were heated.

And she knew—she *knew*—sex with Lincoln would be so good.

"We'll fight it. Business only," she said.

"No pleasure," he added, his eyes back on her mouth.

She licked it—not meaning to.

He swore low in his throat.

"Deal?" she asked, removing her hand from his wrist where the pounding of his pulse revealed the fast beating of his heart.

"Deal," Lincoln agreed.

She picked up her flute and raised it to him a bit.

He did the same.

And they toasted to all business and no pleasure.

Four

One week later

In the rear of the SUV Lincoln glanced over at Bobbie who was staring out the tinted window at the streets of New York as the vehicle moved forward at a good pace. She had her wavy hair pulled back from her face with a thin black elastic band and large black shades in place. She wore a formfitting tee that exposed her belly with torn and tattered jeans that hung low on her hips, topped with a fringed scarf loosely tied around her neck, a thin blazer and then an oversized wool trench with the collar up.

Just effortlessly sexy.

What is she thinking?

Over the last week, they had continued their charade for the Cress family. Bobbie and he joined Phillip

Junior and his wife for an evening of opera in Paris, and game night/drinks with Gabe and Monica aboard the family yacht. A raucous time at an upscale gentleman's club with Lucas, and a flight to Vegas for gambling with Sean.

Each time he had Bobbie by his side. His cushion. He had come to enjoy her acerbic sense of humor and quick tongue. Exchanging barbs with her had taken a lighter tone, but her wittiness remained.

And so did his desire for her.

More importantly, somehow over the last week, they forged a friendship and that outweighed his desire to slowly strip off every stitch of clothing and bury his face—

"Where exactly are we going?" she asked, looking across at him.

Lincoln reached over and raised her glasses from her eyes with his finger. "Why the shades?" he asked sardonically.

Bobbie slapped his hand away before pushing the sunglasses atop her head.

He frowned. "I don't get it," he said.

"Trust me—I know you don't," she said before chuckling.

"I thought we called a truce," he said.

And they had.

Even outside their charade for his family, Bobbie had made it her mission to infuse fun into his life as they explored New York during her downtime. They were becoming friends. Without benefits.

"We have," she agreed, biting her bottom lip.

Lincoln's eyes dropped to take in the move. "Bobbie," he warned.

She gave him a wide-eyed innocent look he wasn't quite sure he believed. "What?" she asked.

"Okay," he said. "Play with fire."

"Awwwww. Poor baby. Are my lips your weakness?" she teased, exaggeratedly pouting them.

"Not so much at the moment," he drawled with sarcasm.

She reached to pinch his arm.

"Ow!" he roared, even as he noticed the gap in her blazer reveal she was sans bra beneath her formfitting T-shirt.

"What do you have against brassieres?" he snapped.

Bobbie looked downed and corrected her blazer. "I have on layers. No one but a certain angry Brit who watches me closely would notice," she said.

"Look. Not touch. As agreed," he said, as the SUV slowed at a red light.

Bobbie nodded. "My apologies for teasing. I enjoy seeing your rare lack of composure way too much, Brit," she said, using her new nickname for him.

"Once the door was opened it hasn't been easy pushing *it* back in and keeping the door closed," he admitted, his voice deep and serious.

"It?"

"Wanting you," he admitted, leveling his gaze on hers.

And he saw her take a gasp. Like his admission rattled her. That shook him.

Bobbie nodded and pressed her hand to her throat.

He knew the pulse beneath her touch throbbed. Just like he ached for her.

"We can't," she stressed in a whisper.

Lincoln felt the shift in energy in the vehicle. That

was how it was with them since the dinner at Cole and Jillian's. Everything would be fine and relaxed until a touch or an accidental double entendre would remind them of what they were fighting to ignore. It was the invisible elephant in the room.

He could so clearly see himself grab her by the waist to lift her over onto his lap and kiss her mouth. That mouth. Full and plush. Truly his weakness.

"I know," he finally agreed, letting the tempting imagery fade.

What was it about Bobbie Barnett that was so damn hard to deny?

They both turned their heads to look out their respective windows.

"Are we going to Jersey?" she asked as they took the exit for the Garden State Parkway.

Lincoln cast her a brief look. "Absolutely," he said.

"For?" she asked.

"Wait and see."

They glanced at each other again.

The desire to have her in his arms, snuggled up by his side with her head on his shoulder as they rode, filled him.

Bobbie tilted her head to the side and gave him a chastising look at whatever she saw in his eyes. "Lincoln," she chided him softly.

"What?" he asked.

"We can't. We *won't*," she stressed.

He nodded and clasped his hands together in the air between his knees. Tightly. To keep from reaching for her. "I thought you said I needed great sex in my life?"

Bobbie visibly swallowed over a lump in her throat as she eyed him. "Would it be great?"

"Why wouldn't it?"

She pursed her lips and released a long breath. "Many reasons. No chemistry. You could be a lazy lay. You might be...*deficient* where it counts," she said with an intentional look between his thighs.

Lincoln spread his knees wider. "I promise you I've never gotten complaints about *any* of that."

"Oh wow," she whispered.

"Yes indeed," he promised with a confident look.

Bobbie bit down on the side of her thumb and crossed her legs as she forced herself to look out the window.

Shook.

Just because he couldn't taste her goodies didn't stop him from loving that she wanted him to.

Bzzzzzz. Bzzzzzz. Bzzzzzz.

He withdrew his vibrating phone but placed it on Silent, and slid it back into the pocket of the leather jacket he wore, at the sight of his mother calling. *Not now*, he thought. He enjoyed himself when he was in Bobbie's company and he didn't want it ruined by another of his mother's tirades on his betrayal of her.

"Do you get along with your father?" he asked.

Bobbie smiled and it filled her brown eyes. "He raised me after my mom's death so he's all I had to rely on and he's never let me down, not even when I make choices he doesn't agree with—like expanding the business. He's always supportive—most times," she drawled.

"Lucky you," Lincoln said.

She touched his arm as she slid a little closer to him on the seat and every pulse in his body reacted. "Phillip or your mom?" she asked, her eyes filled with concern.

Lincoln looked at her. He never vented or complained

about either of his parents. Not when Poppy was misbehaving nor when he felt ignored by Phillip for all those years. He kept it all to himself. But Bobbie knew more than most—whether he liked it or not. "I assume you know a little bit about my mum?" he asked.

"Some," she acknowledged with a shift of her eyes away from him.

More than she's willing to admit.

"You met her?" he asked.

Bobbie nodded. "Yes, I did."

"Then you know she's a lot."

"I thought she was fun," she said.

"Yeah! But for her bloody kid she's a lot," he stressed, wiping his hand over his mouth as he worked his jaw to release tension.

"I can see that," Bobbie said.

"I just don't see why me being here for two weeks is such a big deal. Why wouldn't she want that for me? To have a father. Not that I needed him or his money. I'm a grown-ass man, you know? But why does it disturb her so much?"

Bobbie squeezed his forearm, offering comfort. "Fear at losing—whether real or not. The Cress family is also a lot especially for a single mom on a fixed income who relies on a successful son while Phillip Senior can abundantly provide," she said. "Maybe anger that he left—whether true or not—and that she doesn't believe he deserves her great kid's attention after forty-some-odd years."

Lincoln felt some of the tension ease and worked his shoulders to further relax.

"When I interviewed your mother for the *article*," she said with air quotes. "I can tell you this. She loves her kid. She's proud of him. Wants the best for him. And I think—and I could be wrong because I don't know you people—"

"Don't you," he said sardonically with a side-eye look.

Bobbie bit back a smile. "An-y-way, I think if there is anything Poppy is fighting against for you it is because she honestly believes it's not the best thing for you. It doesn't make her right but it makes her a fierce mama bear looking out for a six-foot-two, broad-shouldered cub. Right?"

Lincoln gave her a look. "Broad shoulders, huh?"

"Focus," she admonished.

"It's hard with your hand on me and you're so close," he said, his eyes dipping to her mouth.

"Lincoln," Bobbie began. "Your mother is doing—and was doing—the best she can as a mother, a woman, a caregiver and someone who may be gripped by disappointment."

He reached to lightly grasp her chin. "Do you know if Phillip Senior knew about me?" he asked, his voice never sounding so serious even to his ears.

Bobbie made sure to match his stare, feeling this was an important question to be answered for him. "Honestly I don't know. It's her word against his, unfortunately. And it's a question you may never get an answer to because who do you believe?"

"Exactly," he agreed, giving her chin a gentle tweak before releasing her to sit back against his seat as he gazed out the window at the factories and retail offices lining the parkway.

She surprised him by capturing one of his hands

between both of hers and shifting closer on the seat to rest her head against his arm.

Just the way he wanted earlier.

Lincoln turned his head and smelled her hair. It was fresh and sweet, like cocoa butter. Her breasts were pressed to his arm and her thigh lined up against his. The fit was ideal.

And arousing.

He moved their hands from the space between his open legs to atop his thigh, afraid any further stirring of his inches would poke her wrist. "Bobbie," he said, his voice as strained as his fight to keep from easing down upon the rear seat to kiss. Deeply. Until he was quenched of the need to feel if her lips were as soft as they looked. "I need a little space. Remember your one-year rule and my return to England in a week."

She shook her head. "No, what you need more at this moment is a friend who sees you're upset. So put on your big boy pants and suffer through it because you are getting this comfort, Lincoln Cress."

It took a few minutes to redirect his thoughts before he relaxed, putting aside both his desire and his wounded feelings about his parents.

They rode that way in silence, with his thumb stroking the side of her hand until the driver pulled the SUV to a stop. It was then he heard her gentle snores. "We're here, Bobbie," he said, shaking her awake.

She softly grunted and smacked those lips as she raised her head to peer out the window with eyes still filled with sleep. She frowned. "The Jersey Shore?" she asked. "But it's cold."

The driver was opening the rear door by the time she cleared her head, replaced the ankle boots Lincoln didn't know she removed and slid her crossbody bag over her head. "Thank you," she said to the chauffeur.

Lincoln looked at the boardwalk up ahead and a large roller coaster in the distance. "I've never ridden one," he admitted. "Never had time. Took on way too many responsibilities and hardly was a kid. Well, today is the day."

"Well, I've never been on one either, but I'm scared of heights, so today is most definitely not the day!" Bobbie said, turning to reopen the rear door of the SUV.

Lincoln rushed to step in front of her. "All week long you have dragged me across this city feeding me food—"

"You *loved* that chop cheese sandwich," she said of the New York bodega staple of chopped meat cooked down with onions on a hero roll with melted cheese, lettuce and tomato.

"Yes, but not the sketchy neighborhood so much," he said with wide eyes.

Bobbie flung her head back and laughed. "You were with me," she said. "I'm trained in combat fighting."

Lincoln looked pensive. "First, I promise you I can handle myself," he told her. "Second. A combat fighter, huh?"

Bobbie playfully curled her lip and curled her arm to make a fist. "Absolutely," she said.

"You get on the ride with me and then I will spar with you," he said, extending his hand.

She sized him up with her eye twinkling with unleashed laughter. "I've taken down bigger," she forewarned.

"But not better."

The laughter faded from her eyes to be replaced by

heat. "Are we still talking about combat?" she asked, her tone husky.

Lincoln said nothing and just dropped his head even as he kept his dark and intense eyes locked on her.

"I am *so* curious if you are as good in bed as you imply," she said. "With your hard body and bowlegged walk as if your thighs are not allowed to touch because of *it*. I want to. More than I have wanted to be in a really long time. But I won't. Nope."

"And are you as good as you imply with your wild hair and juicy mouth? Your style begs to be seen. With even the slightest movement of your body screaming *hot sex*. Like it's held up inside you ready to burst at any moment, waiting for the right one to pull the string and free it," he said.

Her chest rose and fell with a deep breath that revealed she was trying to steady herself. To fight that thing constantly teasing and taunting them. The promise of chemistry. Passion. Heat.

Maybe just once...

"I don't know. I'm just being me. My ex didn't think so," she said.

He saw the flash of pain in her eyes and wanted to punish the man who put it there. "He's a fool."

"Yes," she agreed. "Let me say *this*. I'm not a divorced woman blaming herself for his actions. I'm not looking in the mirror searching for what I did wrong or what I could have done differently. Nothing...except not trust someone who didn't deserve to be trusted. That's about him. Not me. *That* I know. O-kay?"

He admired that spunk. That confidence. That self-awareness and self-love. He liked it a lot.

Over the years he had seen his mother nearly destroyed by a breakup.

Bobbie was cut from a different cloth. She had the power to excite his desire and soothe his anger without much effort. She had shown the wisdom of elders, the strength of a warrior and the vulnerability of a woman who had opened herself to love.

They fell in step with each other as they made their way down the boardwalk and over to the roller coaster. It was still early in the amusement park season, normally not started until summer on the East Coast because the spring weather could be chilly. There was just a short line of people waiting to board the ride. Lincoln had found one of a few in the area opened for business.

"I can't believe you talked me into this," she said, looking nervous as they took their seat together and were strapped in place securely.

"I risked my life for a chop cheese," he reminded her. "You can do this."

"Bloody hell," she said, mimicking his British accent as the roller coaster lurched forward.

Lincoln reached for her hand and she gladly grasped his tightly as she pressed her eyes closed and squealed through the entire ride, every turn and upside-down loop that nearly stopped her heart.

The ride paused.

"Open your eyes and enjoy the view, Bobbie," Lincoln urged.

Still breathing heavily she shook her head to deny him.

"Trust me, please," he added with warmth.

Her grip on his hand tightened as she slowly opened her eyes and looked around at the entire amusement park now beneath where they sat at the top of the roller coaster.

"My legs are trembling," she said, even as her breathing calmed.

"Take a little time to enjoy the view, Bobbie," he urged.

She cut him a side-eye. "Okay, Whoopi Goldberg," she droned, referencing the host of the talk show *The View* and their daily tagline.

"Amusing," he said.

Bobbie arched a brow. "Do you laugh, chuckle, hell, smile?" she asked him in wonder.

"When warranted," was his super-serious reply. "And that's rare."

The roller coaster began to ease forward as she recognized his dry attempt at having fun at her expense. "Go to—"

They accelerated downward.

"Helllllllll," she exclaimed as it transformed to a yell.

Bobbie looked over Lincoln's broad shoulder as they danced along the edge of the ballroom of the luxury Midtown hotel. Her eyes were locked on her target, the wife of her client who suspected she was cheating with his business partner and best friend. The woman was a sexy blonde with waist-length hair that she smoothly flipped back over her shoulder as she looked up at the tall and handsome redheaded man with whom she danced.

"You look beautiful, Bobbie," Lincoln said in a low voice near her ear.

She shivered. She couldn't help herself. "Thank you," she said with a lick of her lips.

Bobbie wore a black strapless jumpsuit of lightweight wool with wide legs with a fitted waist giving the silhouette of a dress until she moved and revealed differently. She did pull her hair back into a tight ponytail to avoid it drawing attention while she was undercover.

Lincoln eased his hand to her bared lower back.

Bobbie leaned back a bit to look up at him. "You joined me on this stakeout to help, not to distract," she said, as he made his finger dance up her spine.

Her body was his puppet, reacting to him with swiftness. Goose bumps covered her skin and her nipples hardened.

"Then I should tell you the target is leaving," he said, with a lift of his square chin in that direction.

Bobbie looked back over her shoulder. "Turn us," she ordered.

He did.

Over Lincoln's shoulder, the wife and the business partner of her client had separated to cross the ballroom, but both were headed to exits.

"Was the husband right?" Lincoln asked.

Her client had orchestrated the night. He was purposefully away on a business trip and had encouraged his wife to attend the event knowing his business partner would be there as well.

"Let's find out," she said, stopping to wrap her arm around his as they followed the wife out of the ballroom.

The target continued down the ornately decorated hallway to the lobby where she briefly stopped at the front desk to talk to the staff before continuing to the elevator.

"Wow. They're bold," Lincoln said.

"I've seen worse," she told him.

When the target paused and glanced back over her shoulder before stepping on the elevator, Lincoln pulled Bobbie close and bent his head to press his lips down on hers.

Bobbie stiffened for a brief moment before melting in his embrace and desperately gripping his strong forearms in the black tuxedo he wore.

Oh, he feels good.

Lincoln broke the kiss just as Bobbie longed for the addition of his tongue. "What now?"

"What?" she asked, opening her eyes as she still clung to him.

The look on his face was a little smug. "That wasn't even a real kiss," he boasted.

"Not at all," she scoffed.

Liar.

Just the feel of his lips, his touch and his tight embrace had her nervous the steps she took to walk would result in a stagger.

Bobbie cleared her throat and walked over to press the button to call for another elevator. Lincoln came to stand beside her. She eyed their reflection. It was hard to deny they looked good together.

Damn good.

She lightly touched her mouth, longing for more of his kisses. More of him.

"Is she getting away?" he asked.

Bobbie smiled. "The tux has you feeling very James Bond-ish tonight," she teased as the door slid open and she stepped on. "*I'm* the investigator. Remember?"

Lincoln slid one hand into the pocket of his tailored slacks and shrugged one shoulder. "Tonight, *we're* on the case," he countered.

"Suddenly you're okay with minding people's business?" she asked with feigned shock, reminding him of their barb-filled first meeting.

Lincoln clenched his jaw as he stared ahead. "The man deserves to know if his wife is on the pull."

"On—on the pull?" Bobbie asked in confusion.

Lincoln released a breath as the elevator slowed to a stop. "Looking for sex" he explained, stepping back so that she could exit first.

Ever the gentleman.

"I would think *wanting to pull* is better. Don't you?" she asked, opening her clutch as they walked down the length of the hall where the luxury was just as evident as every other part of the Fifth Avenue five-star hotel decorated in French Renaissance.

She glanced up at him.

Lincoln's face was deadpan.

"One day I *will* make you smile," she declared.

"Doubtful."

She just laughed.

"How do you know where she went?" he asked, pausing to look up and down the length of the hall.

Bobbie continued down the corridor with a satisfied look on her face before she opened the feather-covered clutch she carried and removed a key card. She stopped in front of a door and unlocked it, motioning with her finger for him to be quiet and to follow her into the guest room.

He did.

She looked on as he closed the door behind him before continuing down the hall, past the open double doors of the luxurious bathroom into the bedroom. At the foot of the king-size bed were a love seat and a small padded ottoman serving as a coffee table. Bobbie sat on the sofa looking at two laptops open atop the dresser. On them were the videos from the two mini surveillance cameras she'd already placed in the hall earlier.

"She booked the room earlier today and I booked this one beside her," she finally explained as he took the seat next to her.

His thigh was pressed along hers.

Bobbie tried her best to ignore it. Tried and failed. Off her pulse went with speed.

"Don't tell me you have a surveillance *inside* her suite?" Lincoln asked, his voice hard and accusing.

Bobbie turned her head to look out the window, feeling an awakening of her resentment of him from their early days. "Regardless of your insults and low thinking of me, I move a bit differently from how private detectives are portrayed in movies. I have a line—actually many lines—I don't cross, Lincoln," she said, trying not to show that her feelings were hurt. "It is that integrity that I'm known for. I could burst with the secrets I'm keeping, but it is necessary to do *that*."

"Hey," Lincoln said with softness, pressing a hand to her back.

This time his touch was irksome and she shook it off.

"My bad, Bobbie," he said, his breath caressing her neck. "I made a wrong assumption. I apologize."

Her body softened at his regret. "Lincoln Cress apologize?" she teased.

In the reflection of the window, she saw him reach toward her face so his fingers touching her chin didn't startle her, but that switch in her body that controlled her reaction to him was flipped on. He guided her face so that they looked at one another. Separated by just inches but with metaphorical miles and miles of deep desire between them.

"I'm sorry," he stressed with earnestness.

The air was so charged. *So* electrifying. Bobby felt heady from it. She nodded her acceptance and quickly jumped to her feet, needing the distance between them before she was completely drawn in by his magnetism. And it was all physical and inherent because Lincoln was far from a charmer—*handsome* but stoic and serious and sometimes stiff. Although there was a hint that beneath that was straight fire and she was longing more and more to be scorched.

Maybe we can set a date for ten months from today...

Bobbie sat on the edge of the bed and looked over at Lincoln's profile.

I want to suck his mouth, his fingers and his—

"He's at the door," Lincoln said, glancing back at her before refocusing his gaze on the laptops.

Bobbie slid her hand into the pocket of her pants as she crossed the room to stand by where Lincoln still sat on the love seat. "Of course. She was ready and waiting," she said, having mixed feelings that her instincts had been correct but she had bad news to deliver to her client.

Another affair.

They looked on as the couple shared a long and hot kiss in the doorway before he wrapped an arm around her waist and carried her inside to slam the door shut.

Lincoln looked up at her and Bobbie was unable to look away.

There in the depths of their eyes was the awareness of the passion the couple would share right next door and how they both yearned to have that with each other. Revealing further that they shared that longing they both glanced at the bed quickly and then back at each other.

"What now?" Lincoln asked.

Strip.

"Huh?" Bobbie asked, pushing aside the image of him doing just that.

"You have proof they're shagging," Lincoln said. "What happens now?"

"I hang around to see when he—or they—leave," she explained, kicking off her heels. "Sometimes it's all night. But this one won't be. My client knows she is expecting a call from him to their mansion house phone at midnight."

"Just a quickie then?" Lincoln asked, looking at his designer watch.

"You don't have to wait," she said, as she picked up the room's tablet to order room service.

"I'm your ride," he reminded her.

"I can Uber."

"I'm not ready to go back to the town house yet," was his return as he rose and walked over to look down at the à la carte menu.

"Isn't that why you're even in the country...and why we're hanging out? For *them*?" Bobbie asked as she used the tip of her glossy almond-shaped nail to run down the items listed.

"Things changed," he said simply.

Bobbie didn't dare to look up at him. Not with her body excited by his closeness and his words—and everything they implied. "You've been with me all day."

"Most I've enjoyed my time in New York."

That surprised her. "How would I know that when

your only expression all day was stern or frowning?" she asked.

"I didn't complain."

True. He had not.

"You don't have to worry about wrinkles," she said dryly.

He gave her a slight shrug with a minute incline of his head.

And what face do you make when you climax?

"Hungry?" she asked, motioning to him with the tablet.

She paused and closed her eyes, hearing how that one-word question could be taken in another way. "For food," she rushed to add, hearing the tremble of nerves in her voice.

Lincoln snorted.

Bobbie whirled. "Was that a chuckle?" she asked, her eyes wide in astonishment.

"Definitely not," he drawled.

She gave her attention back to the tablet and quickly ordered porcini-crusted filet mignon served with creamed spinach and potatoes cooked in foie gras.

"Order me something too, Bobbie," Lincoln requested.

She did, before walking over to show him the tablet. "I'm curious. What would you have picked?" she asked.

He yawned. "Whatever you picked is fine."

"Yes, but what would you have picked?" she insisted.

"Fine," he said, eyeing the tablet. "The fennel-dusted salmon."

"Yes! That's what I got you," Bobbie exclaimed as she turned to set the tablet back atop the side table by the bed. "Just checking on my instincts."

Suddenly Lincoln's arms came around her from behind in a bear hug. "What do your instincts say now?" he asked.

Oh. Really?

And with three swift moves in rapid succession, she bent her knees, raised her hands hard to jerk up his arms and moved sideways to free herself. To seal the deal, she gave two more swift moves that landed the sizable man on the floor beneath her with her forearm pressed under his chin.

"Impressive," he said.

Bobbie's breaths were a bit heavy from the exertion as she looked down into Lincoln's face. Studied it and missed absolutely nothing. Not even the small flat mole on his cheek. The single gray hair in his goatee. His long lashes. And his mouth that he kept in a frown or thin line was…was…tempting.

And just one dip of her head away.

A couple of inches, if that.

So close.

She raised her eyes from his mouth to his eyes. With her upper body pressed down upon his chest and a gleam of pure intense raw desire in his eyes, Bobbie felt the breath she took slow as she fought for control.

Of her body.

Her desire.

The need to kiss him. Taste him. Have him.

You can't. You can't.

Then Lincoln reached up to free her hair and entwine his fingers through the waves as he pulled her head down to his.

Bobbie gasped softly.

The anticipation was intoxicating and not to be denied.

The first feel of his tongue flicking against her mouth was the beginning and the end of her resistance. Her entire body felt a spark like nothing ever before.

Ever.

She trembled as she tumbled face-first into passion. Heart-pounding, pulse-racing, mind-blowing passion as the bud nestled between the lips of her core ached seeking an explosive release.

It was exhilarating. New. Different. Addictive.

"Lincoln," she sighed just before he deepened the kiss with a guttural moan.

Like he was starving for her.

She understood his hunger and matched it with her own, wrapping her arms around his neck and clinging to him as she succumbed to a desire to be fed.

Five

We're doing this.

Bobbie's tongue tangoed with Lincoln's as he turned their bodies on the floor until she was pressed beneath him. As she wrapped her legs around his waist, his thick hardness snaked against her swollen and pulsing bud. She moaned, arching her back as Lincoln shifted to press hot kisses down the length of her throat. He deeply suckled her pulse point and she bit down on her bottom lip to quiet a shrill cry of pleasure from escaping.

She gave in, releasing a long and shaky breath through pursed lips as she slid herself up against the smooth floor above her head. The echo of him undoing the side zipper of her jumpsuit blended with her purrs. She looked at him as he lowered the top, leaving her breasts free for his to enjoy. He shook his head as if in wonder before easing both hands around her waist and raising her upper body with her head tilted back and her hair skimming the floor.

"Damn," he swore before lowering his head to lick each of her taut nipples.

Bobbie didn't deny the cry of pleasure. She couldn't. He drew it from her with ease as he sucked her flesh and buried his head in the cleavage with a deep and guttural moan. "Lincoln," she gasped. "Lincoln!"

He cut his penetrating eyes up at her as he sucked nearly the whole of one of her breasts into his mouth as he twirled the nipple with his tongue.

Shaking her head, she covered her face with both of her hands feeling pushed over the edge at the very sight of the pleasure he gave. She craved him but the pleasure was so intense she was afraid of it as well. As if insanity was just a blink away. Never had she felt close to madness. She was a trembling and throbbing mess as he laid her back against the floor before roughly removing the jumpsuit.

She opened her eyes just as he flung it over his head and then grabbed her lace thong in his fist to tear it away as he sat on his knees between her legs. She spread them wider as she reached to cup her breasts and tease her nipples.

"Bobbie!" he gasped, rushing out of his tuxedo jacket and nearly ripping off the bow tie before undoing the zip and button of his pants to free his hard length.

Stroking it from thick root to thick tip. Slight curve and all.

Even the sight of him removing a condom from his wallet and sheathing himself thrilled her.

She kept her eyes locked on his dark expression as she moved her hands down to stroke her damp bud.

The first feel of her fingers made her hiss and moan. He locked on the move, tilting his head to the left to watch her as he furrowed his brows and released a low whistle that made her release a soft laugh.

Lincoln stretched out on the floor and raised her legs high in the air to bury his head between them. The first lick of his tongue against her core turned her thighs to Jell-O as they quivered. Blindly, she reached out and cupped the back of his head as he feasted. Licked. Sucked.

The taste of her was everything he had dreamed of over the last week. Everything and more. Sweet smelling and clean tasting.

He released her bud from between his lips with the sound of a pucker as he looked down at her femininity laid out before him. The sweet nestle of her lips, her core and the fleshy bud that glistened and begged for more of his attention.

He felt wild. He lowered his head and tongued her again, enjoying the feel of her trembles and her cries. Enjoying her release on his tongue and lips. He fought for control to not be anxious or too wild with her driven by his desire to be inside her. Deeply.

With his heart beating in unison to the vein pulsing along the length of his firm inches he looked up at her, his breathing ragged.

"I want you *inside* me," she said, almost pleading with him.

As if she had to.

Lincoln gave her bud one last lick and deep suck before he eased his body atop hers. He kissed her deeply and when she sucked the taste of her juices from his tongue that shattered the last of his resolve. Reasoning was gone. Nothing mattered in that moment but pleasure. Satiation. Release.

He rose to look down at her, enraptured by the sight of her eyes glossy with desire, and her mouth parted with each breath as her wild hair was splayed out. "So damn beautiful," he stressed before lowering his head to press kisses to the mouth that drove him to distraction. It was soft and plush. There was the slight taste of chocolate in her lip gloss adding sweetness to the heat they created.

He desired her. Wanted her. And at that moment, he *needed* her. No other woman could sate the hunger she had stoked in him all week.

They were too far to turn back.

Lincoln bit down upon her shoulder as he bent his back to thrust inside her with one hard stroke. He stiffened at the feel of her and dug his face deeply against the crook of her neck as he willed himself not to spill his seed.

She was tight and wet and her grasp, as she clung to his body, spoke to her liking the feel of him. He felt her walls pulsing against him as they gripped his length like a fist. The heat of her against his sensitive tip made his body tremble as he clutched her buttocks. He fought the feeling to glide inside her wetness.

Not yet. He wasn't ready.

"Please," she whispered against his neck as she slid her hands beneath the edge of his crisp white tuxedo shirt to grip his waist. "I need this. I need this so bad. I'm aching."

Bobbie pressed against his chest and turned their bodies again until she was astride him, sliding down the few inches he held back until he was fully rooted inside her. Lincoln's mouth shaped the letter O and he gripped her hips, digging his fingers into her fleshy buttocks as she rode him. Fast and hard. Furious even.

All he could do was sit back and enjoy the ride as she took control, circling her hips and pressing her hands down upon his chest as she flung her hair back from her face. Her breasts bounced up and down with each back-and-forth motion of her hips as she slid up and down his inches.

The sight and feel of her were glorious.

An uncontrolled shot of his seed filled her.

She gasped and stopped. "I felt that," she whispered down to him as she bent to suck the tip of his tongue into her mouth.

Lincoln eased his arms under her thighs to lift her body high, giving him the room to pump upward into her.

"Ah!" she cried into his mouth.

He was relentless, building up a sweat and pushing himself to the brink of sanity for the thrill of feeling and seeing her response. Uninhibited. Raw. Real.

He bit his bottom lip and pummeled away. Swift and deep.

Bobbie reached to gather her hair into her fists as her head fell back exposing her throat while she screamed out with her release coating his inches.

That broke him. He wanted to join her in the bliss. Desperately.

"Damn!" he roared with a grimace as he gave in to the waves with deep thrusts that soon broke down as he felt the pleasure of it all would drive him to madness.

* * *

They both lay on the floor releasing harsh and ragged breaths that filled the air.

Oh no. Oh no. Oh no. Oh no.

Bobbie covered her eyes with her forearms as her fleshy bud continued to pulse in the aftermath. She pressed her thighs together but that did nothing to stop it. "What on God's green earth have I *done*?" she howled.

Lincoln's body went stiff beside her. She climbed up off the floor to her bare feet.

"On. The. *Floor*," she wailed, before rushing around the room to pick up her clothing to dump on the middle of the bed.

"While working, I might add," she said, making a motion with her hand.

At Lincoln's continued silence, she glanced back to find him sitting on the floor with his elbows propped atop his knees. Pants and boxers still down around his ankles. Shoes on. His member now flaccid against his thigh.

Fresh from a hot and spicy quickie.

On the floor!

She pinched the bridge of her nose as she reached for her clutch and removed a small citrine crystal. She stepped up onto the middle of the bed and sat cross-legged with the crystal gripped in one hand as she began to inhale and exhale slowly, forcing herself to relax. "I give myself permission to start again with my healing," she said in a soft voice as she visualized light surrounding and flowing through her body.

"What is this about?" Lincoln drawled, sounding closer.

She opened one eye, finding him standing by the side

of the bed and zipping up his pants. "A spiritual cleansing," she said. "I am replacing the negative energy of guilt and disappointment with myself with the healing light of forgiveness and a fresh start."

Lincoln snorted.

The urge to toss the crystal at his head was *very* strong.

"Looks like he's leaving," Lincoln said.

Bobbie's eyes shot to the laptop as her client's best friend left with a smug and toothy grin. She rushed over to stand beside Lincoln.

"He looks satisfied," he quipped.

She gave him a side-eye. "So do you," she drawled.

"Absolutely," he agreed with a nod. He looked down at her before giving her body a hot look of pure appreciation. "And you're not?"

Completely satisfied. She could sleep her life away she was so relaxed. She tore her gaze from him as she pushed away thoughts of what a long night with him would be like. Opening her hand, she looked down at the yellow crystal in it. "I really am disappointed I broke my promise," she admitted with softness as tears rose and blurred her vision.

Lincoln used his index finger to raise her head as he studied her with dark eyes. "We were fooling ourselves to think we could fight it," he said.

Bobbie crossed her arms over her chest as her nipples hardened in awareness. Her body was not done with him. Even as she was assailed by guilt and regret, clutching a crystal, she wanted him again. "Yes, we were," she admitted with a woeful shake of her head.

Lincoln pulled her close for a hug. "We got it out of

our systems. Let's shift back to just friends—no matter how *good* the sex," he said.

"*Sooooo* good," she agreed in amazement. "Whoooo."

"Bobbie."

She glanced up at him. "Hmm?"

"Could you get dressed?"

"I'm not ashamed of my nudity," she said. "Most times I find clothing restrictive."

"You're a nudist?"

"In private? *Yes*," she stressed.

"You have no reason to be ashamed. Your body is amazing," he emphasized, releasing her to take a step back. "But unless you want me to lay you in the middle of that bed and make more regret, please put on some damn clothes."

"Oh!" she said in sudden realization. "Right. Just friends. No benefits. Not even my amazing body."

Lincoln turned, but not before she spotted his arousal straining against his pants.

Ready for round two in minutes? Wow.

"Impressive," she muttered with raised brows as she grabbed her jumpsuit to pull it back on.

Lincoln pointed to the screen of the laptop. "She's headed home."

They looked on as the target emerged from the suite fully dressed and composed as if a steamy tryst had not occurred behind locked doors. "That's that then," Bobbie said, turning off the cameras and closing the laptops. "One guilty wife about to be served up."

"How do you know if the husband isn't cheating too or does it matter?" Lincoln asked as Bobbie stepped into her heels.

"Most wouldn't, but to be honest before I begin

working on a new case I do a little intel on my client," she admitted, opening her clutch and placing her small crystal back inside it. "Just to make sure I'm not getting pulled into something unaware or being lied to and manipulated."

"The B. Barnett difference," Lincoln added.

She glanced over at him. "You a chef or adman?" she asked. "Because I may have to use that."

"Feel free."

They shared a glance and just like that the unseen chemistry was back pressing between them and attempting to push them to be together.

With regret, they turned away from each other, obviously determined to ignore the enticement and not make the same mistake twice.

Lincoln hummed as he strolled into the dining room of the town house the next morning. He paused when all eyes rested on him in open surprise and curiosity. He frowned. "Good morning," he said as he continued to his normal seat between Sean and Lucas across from Collette sitting between her parents.

He had barely poured himself a cup of aromatic Brazilian coffee when Chef Carlisle entered with a plate in hand that he soon set down in from of him. "A little piece of home," Lincoln said, eyeing the full English breakfast, or fry-up, of sausage, bacon, poached egg, baked beans, grilled tomatoes, mushrooms and toast.

As a chef, Lincoln could tell Chef Carlisle had put his twist on many of the traditional British items just by look and smell, elevating it beyond normal fare. He didn't doubt the sausage, beans and bread were homemade. He had learned during his brief time at the town house that the chef was just as talented and passionate about his craft as himself. Serving as the personal chef to the acclaimed Cress family of culinary elites would take nothing less.

"Ton Oncle Lincoln est heureux," Collette declared as she dipped her sausage in the baked beans.

"I'm always happy," Lincoln said, using his fork and knife to cut the yolk of his egg.

Sean nudged his arm. "You do seem lighter," he agreed. "More relaxed."

Lincoln just shrugged, but he thought of Bobbie— and not just the explosive sex they shared the night before—but her positivity and lighthearted nature that was infectious. He truly enjoyed just being in her company. Just feeling their attraction pulse between them even as they fought it had been enticing.

Until they had given in to it.

And then it was explosive.

"We need to take the jet back to Vegas and have fun this time," Sean offered before dragging his toast in his runny yolk.

"You had plenty of fun," Lincoln drawled, cutting his sausage and fighting the urge as a chef filled with endless passion and curiosity about food to sniff the meat to help detect its ingredients. He also served his version of the fry-up with the addition of hog's pudding and potatoes cooked to a crisp in butter. "But I was thinking I would cook dinner for the whole family. I want to show you all that I did inherit the Cress cooking genes."

Lincoln took a bite of the sausage. He grunted in pleasure. It was seasoned well with the right consistency. He picked up subtle notes of sage and garlic.

The reaction reminded him of last night with Bobbie when he suckled her bud.

Sex and food. Two of the world's greatest wonders. He enjoyed both vigorously. Relished them.

He paused before his next bite remembering the taste and feel of her in his mouth. He grunted again.

Magnificent.

"I was checking out your website for SHORES," Sean said. "I really like what you're doing with sustainability."

Lincoln washed down his food with a deep sip of coffee. "Thanks. I'm dedicated to reducing waste and being more mindful of using local ingredients, purchasing food in season, adjusting the design of the kitchen," he explained. "It's become a passion of mine. Over the last year, we've reduced the restaurant's carbon footprint by more than twenty-five percent."

Sean looked thoughtful as he wiped his mouth with a linen napkin. "Maybe we should do an episode on sustainability," he said. "I think my fans would love it."

The third eldest Cress brother was the host of several cooking shows produced by Cress, INC. on several food-centered channels and streaming services. It made him a bona fide food star and celebrity chef with a huge social media following and a couple of inclusions on *People Magazine*'s Sexiest Chef Alive list. He was well loved and well aware of it.

"And what will you be preparing, Lincoln?" Nicolette asked, her French accent ever present.

"Seafood, mostly. At home, I go every morning and catch the day's protein. Fish. Crabs. Lobster," he explained, even as he noticed her plate of food was nearly untouched.

Her blue eyes dipped down to her plate, following his line of vision. She settled her napkin atop the meal. "It's not called a *full* breakfast for nothing," she said with a hesitant smile.

"Think bigger than just an episode," Phillip Senior interjected, his voice stern as his eyes bored into Sean.

"A Cress network station then?" Sean asked before taking a bite, casting their father a brief look, as he shifted his food around on his platinum-rimmed plate.

"Realistically," Phillip Senior insisted.

Lincoln cleared his throat and refilled his coffee cup during their exchange. It was awkward—at least for him. He had come to discover that their father ruled with an iron fist and lacked tolerance for difference of thought. Although his sons respected him, beneath the surface he sensed resentment.

It reminded him of his interactions with his staff and seeing a lot of his father in himself. *That* was a lot to digest.

Sean set back in his chair and bent his leg to settle his ankle atop his knee. "I think diversifying into owning a food network channel is smart *and* profitable," he persisted.

"You've made that very clear," Phillip said, his face filled with his frustration. "And I suppose you want to star in all of them."

Sean flashed his charming smile that millions of viewers adored, but said, "Of course not."

Nicolette chuckled. "I think your father was speaking of creating an executive position for Lincoln at Cress, INC. centered on sustainability…if he decided to join us at the business."

Phillip Junior's fork made a racket as he dropped it from his hand. Everyone ignored him.

Lincoln sat up straighter. "At all the restaurants?" he asked, far beyond intrigued at such an impact that could make with the company owning eleven restaurants across the world.

"Yes. Also, the kitchen at the offices and the cooking school as well. *Oui?*" she said, looking down the length of the large table at her husband.

"Yes, that's right," he answered.

"And that's great," Sean said. "But the channel is a good idea. Cole, Gabe *and* Lucas agree."

"Thanks," Lucas drawled sarcastically.

"Well, I don't agree," Phillip Junior asserted, always seeking their father's favor.

Felice stepped into the dining room. Her face was pained and her eyes landed on Lincoln, offering apologies.

His gut clenched.

Something's wrong.

Lincoln thought of his mother and then Bobbie, feeling alarm wash over him.

"Yes, Felice?" Nicolette asked.

At her continued silence, Phillip Senior twisted his large frame in his chair to stare at her pointedly.

"Paparazzi are outside," she said in a rush with the words nearly colliding with each other.

Phillip Senior released an expletive.

Nicolette shot to her feet in a rare crack in her cool facade. She cast a hard stare at Sean. *"Qu'avez-vous fait maintenant, M. Célébrité?"* she snapped with fiery eyes as she asked him what have you done now.

Sean's expression was as if *many* things could be possible.

She waved her hand at him in disgust as she moved over to the window to ease back the gray velvet curtain. She gasped in horror. "There must be a dozen or more of them, Phillip," she said with a heavy breath.

Lincoln's feeling of doom had not eased. His body went stiff. "It's me. Isn't it, Felice?" he asked the housekeeper.

All heads swiveled in her direction.

She nodded as she removed a television remote from the pocket of her apron to turn on the TV over the fireplace in the den on the other side of the chef kitchen.

Lincoln dropped his fork as well, at the split screen of his and Phillip Senior's headshot.

"There's certainly a resemblance," the male gossip reporter said. *"Ladies and gents, it seems the Cress brothers are five no more. The addition of the illegitimate heir, Lincoln Cress, makes six!"*

"Mon dieu!" Nicolette gasped.

Phillip Senior's face was grim.

Is he ashamed of me?

Lincoln's grip on his coffee cup tightened as photos of his restaurant were displayed as his life was dissected.

"Question is—What does acclaimed chef Nicolette Lavoie-Cress think of her newly discovered stepson... and was this a secret Phillip kept from her?"

Nicolette gave her husband a brief look and shake of her hand.

"Turn it off!" Phillip Senior demanded.

Lincoln had also noticed that his stepmother held her emotions in check and revealed little to nothing in front of the staff or guests—except to demand respect and decorum. Today the veil had slipped and he was sure that angered her further.

"As you know, the lauded Cress family has been the subject of lots of press of late, beginning with their former housekeeper—and future daughter-in-law— Monica Darby, who worked for them without knowing she was the illegitimate heir of a reported fifty-million-dollar inheritance from A-list movie star Brock Maynard. The scandals just seem to keep on coming—"

Felice fumbled the remote before finally turning off the television and leaving the room.

Everything was still. Even Collette looked around at the strained expressions of all the adults, sensing something wrong.

Lincoln was livid at the invasion of his privacy.

"They didn't show your press photo this time, Sean. You okay?" Lucas teased.

"Shocked, but okay," Sean answered with feigned seriousness.

Sean was a bit self-centered, driven by publicity and, at times, insufferable about his popularity, but he was also funny, self-deprecating, smart and talented.

Lincoln liked him. A lot.

"Enough," Phillip Senior demanded firmly.

Sean gave Lucas, the youngest Cress brother, a playful wink.

"I hope this isn't the handiwork of the pretty little PI?" Nicolette said.

"Who *else*?" Phillip asked as he blamed Lincoln with his eyes.

Lincoln looked across the table to stare first at him and then his stepmother. He hid none of his anger at them accusing Bobbie. He felt protective of her like a warrior.

"Nicolette," Phillip Senior interceded before Lincoln could say anything to defend his beautiful friend. "Once I discovered we were investigated by a detective, I asked around about her and her reputation is above par."

"Does *anyone* respect privacy?" Lincoln asked, dropping his napkin onto his plate before striding around the table.

"Uncle Lincoln," Collette called after him.

He paused his steps and turned as she came over to him. Today, her glasses were orange. He softened his face as he stooped down to match her eye level. She wrapped her arms around his neck and pressed a sticky kiss to his cheek by his ear.

"Mon professeur dit qu'être en colère n'est qu'une raison de ne pas être heureux," she whispered to him.

She'd said, "My teacher says that being mad is just a reason not to be happy."

It was adorable. And something Bobbie would say.

Lincoln rested his head on her little shoulder for a moment with just the slightest hint of a smile.

"Merci beaucoup," he said, thanking her as he hugged her briefly before he stood and turned to continue out of the room.

Bobbie released a breath and a small moan as she remembered the feel of Lincoln's mouth on her. Licking. Kissing. Sucking.

The memory was vivid and evoked a thrill.

And then his hardness inside her. Stroke after stroke after stroke. Deeper with each thrust.

The inches.

The hardness.

The climaxes.

Over and over.

He was *the best* she ever had.

"What do you think about it, boss?"

Bobbie cut her eyes down the length of the conference table where her entire staff of private investigators sat looking at her. On the monitor in the corner were the detectives running her twelve satellite offices in DC, California, Florida, Texas, Canada, Hawaii, England, France, Mexico, Nigeria, China and Italy. The team left behind for her to lead was made up of skilled investigators with the majority being former police detectives and ex-agents with the FBI, DEA, IRS and Secret Service.

"Think about what, Rick?" she asked, sitting up straight in her chair and reclaiming her focus.

"Toa was mentioning she knows of an agency in Dubai whose owner is interested in coming under the B. Barnett umbrella," Rick explained.

She eyed the portly man with silver hair who had worked with her father for more than a dozen years as his right-hand man. And now he was hers. She trusted him without fail.

With a shift of her gaze, she took in Toa, the regal dark-skinned beauty with her hair in long thin braids over one shoulder. She was as fierce as she was attractive and flourished with the support of B. Barnett Investigations to tackle cases investigating violent crime and human trafficking in West Africa.

"Toa, your last quarter was amazing," Bobbie said.

"Thank you," she responded with a smile and nod.

"Dubai is intriguing," Bobbie admitted. "Send Ms.

Pott a dossier on the firm and let me do some research to make sure they're a good fit. We'll table this until the next meeting."

"Excellent," Toa agreed.

Bobbie forced a smile. "I think you all can see I'm distracted today. My apologies for that. If there's anything amiss I will be in the office all day today so reach out to me. Okay? Okay."

As everyone rose and either went into their office or left the building, Bobbie leaned back in her chair at the head of the table and stretched her body with her arms wide and her eyes closed.

"Hey. My name is now Cat and I'm curious."

Bobbie chuckled before she looked over at Ms. Pott.

This week her silver hair was tinted light purple. Her personality was as colorful as her hair and she was a fixture at B. Barnett's since the first day her father opened the business. Thankfully she was great at her job and helped keep all the investigators in order with the warmth of a mother's love. She was good as gold and just like family.

"About?" Bobbie finally asked, sitting up straight.

"What's distracting you?" Ms. Pott asked, setting a cup of steaming tea in front of Bobbie before claiming a sip from her own cup.

The front door to the building opened and Lincoln stepped inside.

For Bobbie, his presence changed everything and her body reacted.

"Him," she admitted, as her heart lost its normal beat.

"The Brit?" Ms. Pott asked, also eyeing him from across the room. "He's so rude."

"So are you," Bobbie reminded her.

The older woman rolled her eyes. "I guess he's alright. If you keep his mouth full to shut him up it *might* be fun."

Bobbie gave Lincoln a wave as she stood and smoothed the ivory silk-blend sweater dress she wore. Where the hem stopped at midthighs, her matching leather boots began. "Not might be. *Was.* Most definitely," she said, walking away and leaving a stunned Ms. Pott behind her.

The closer she got to him the more the lines of anger creasing his face became clear.

"What's wrong?" she asked with concern.

"My illegitimacy was just exposed in all the tabloids," he said, his anger clipping his words.

Bobbie winced.

"I'm disgusted," he snapped, wiping his hand over his mouth. "I looked online. It's everywhere. Even the British press. 'The bastard Cress heir' it says."

"Oh, Lincoln," she said, knowing how much he preferred his privacy.

"And then on top of it, Nicolette accused you of selling the story to the rags."

"What!" she exclaimed as she slowly arched a brow.

Lincoln pulled her body to his side for a quick hug that seemed effortless. And natural.

Like he's been doing that forever.

"It's nonsense and I don't believe it," he assured her before releasing her to begin to pace.

"Still offensive as hell," she muttered.

"This is more than I was looking for," he admitted with a rare show of emotion. "I just wanted to meet these people that are my family, not have all of my privacy snatched away. That's *their* life and not mine."

"I understand that, Lincoln. It's a lot to handle," she said, reaching to give his wrist a comforting squeeze.

That too felt natural.

She was surprised when he covered her hand with his own. She liked it. The connection made her entire body tingle with awareness.

"I had to rush through paparazzi to even leave the damn house," he said, focusing his penetrating gaze on her. "I'm heading home early, Bobbie. Today."

Bobbie eased her hand away from him and looked down at her feet to avoid him seeing her eyes. Her regret and sadness. He was scheduled to go home at the end of the week, but she had prepared herself for that. This sudden exit hit her harder than she imagined it would.

Two weeks ago, they disliked each other.

But everything had changed.

Damn.

"Hey," Lincoln said softly as he touched her chin to raise her head. "I just wanted to say goodbye in person and say I was wrong about you in the beginning, Bobbie Barnett. I consider you a friend."

She nodded and forced a smile for his benefit. "Same," she said.

He stroked her chin with his thumb. "And last night was—"

"Is forgotten," she interjected with the biggest lie she would ever tell. "Good…but behind us. Right?"

She extended her hand to him, clinging to formality when she craved to cling to him.

Don't go, Lincoln.

He took her hand into his own and the spark was there. Ever present.

"Right," he agreed, although his eyes said otherwise.

Lincoln raised her hand to his mouth to press a warm kiss to the back of it.

She shivered and released a breath as her heart pounded.

He left with one last lingering look back. Bobbie felt rooted to the spot.

Ms. Pott came up beside her and wrapped an arm around her shoulder. "You okay?" she asked.

Bobbie shook her head. "No. Not at all," she confessed as her eyes watched Lincoln's SUV pull away outside the window.

Six

One month later

Bobbie tapped her stylus against the tablet as she massaged her brow. She was reviewing the files of a robbery cold case and unable to focus—and that was critical to find any clues that could reveal the culprit. She dropped the stylus to run her hands through the loose waves of her hair from root to tip. She smiled, remembering the feel of Lincoln's fingers massaging her scalp before he lightly clutched the wild waves as he deeply kissed her.

Simply amazing.

She softly moaned and bit down on her bottom lip wishing he was there to kiss her some more.

I miss him.

The time since he left had not lessened her feeling the loss of him. Brooding nature and all. During the near two weeks he had been in Manhattan, she had even come to understand his dry sense of humor, enjoyed showing him New York and taken her first ride on a roller coaster because she felt safe beside him.

Together they had fought their attraction and failed. Spectacularly.

It had been nothing like she had ever experienced. The chemistry and the sparks and the explosive firework-type energy were exactly like romance novels and movies. Pure satiation.

And absolutely the last thing she needed in her life.

"You're doing it again," Ms. Pott's voice echoed into her office, said via the intercom.

Bobbie stopped rubbing her scalp and looked through the glass at her office manager eyeing her across the distance. She wore a knowing look—and hair as red as fruit punch. "Doing what exactly?" she asked as if she didn't know.

It had been more than a dozen times that she would massage her scalp, close her eyes and remember Lincoln's kiss, only to discover the older woman watching her with a curious expression.

"Daydreaming," Ms. Pott said. "About the Brit? Maybe I need some older Idris Elba-like company for myself."

During the day Lincoln randomly crossed her mind and sometimes at night he invaded her dreams, leading to her waking up hot, sweaty and aroused. Achingly so. Until she had to pleasure herself to relieve the pressure.

All while thinking of Lincoln watching me with his hard inches in his hand...

Pushing away the erotic recollection, Bobbie picked up her stylus and studied a photo of the crime scene.

"Is there something besides my business that I can help you with, Ms. Pott?" she asked.

"Nope."

Bobbie reached and hit the button on the business phone to turn off the intercom decisively. She picked up her cup of tea for a long sip before trying her best to work to solve the case. Soon, she tossed the stylus and tablet in frustration.

Lincoln Cress was her distraction.

From work. From her newfound peace and balance. From her healing.

Since his return to England, they spoke once a week via FaceTime—about work, something wild his mother did or something scandalous her father said, or the easing of the tabloids in exploiting his paternity. Afterward, she always felt happier—until painful memories of having her joy crushed by her ex's betrayal reminded her that she wasn't done making repairs. She was still putting the broken pieces of her heart back together.

After almost twenty years of marriage, there had been no signs that Henny had been cheating. No late nights. No unanswered calls. No chunks of time where he was unreachable. No dry spells without sex. It truly had been a shock.

When will it stop hurting? When will I get past this?

Unease caused her body to tense. She felt overwhelmed and out of sorts. She splayed her fingers and then balled her hand into a fist as she breathed deeply.

Her heartbreak had led to a focus on her spirituality and although she was still relatively new to it all, she knew such a visceral response to her divorce was a physical manifestation that there was a lesson yet to be learned from it all. Something that would lead to a deeper understanding.

Bobbie turned on her computer and navigated to the YouTube of an intuitive psychic and tarot reader. The young woman had a soothing demeanor and calming energy. While Bobbie's intuition led her to the woman's page, there was always something she connected with and that was so accurate.

Like the spider.

As she was prone to over the years, Bobbie had a time in her life when she was preoccupied with thoughts of her deceased mother on and off for a week or so. Early one morning she was up using the restroom and a small spider came walking toward her. Bobbie had thought nothing about it until the next day when she was online watching funny skit videos on YouTube and saw one of the next videos cued to play had the title PICK A CARD. MESSAGE FROM YOUR SPIRIT GUIDE. Bobbie clicked on it and after following the instructions on asking her spirit guide to lead her to choose one of the three piles of tarot cards, her mind had been blown that the intuitive had mentioned spiders as a symbol that a female figure in her life was deceased and was now her guardian angel.

Bobbie had been so desperate for a connection to her mother and desiring healing from heartbreak that she wasn't one-hundred-percent sure any of it was true but she kept her curiosity. Any time she ventured to one of those videos, she had always found a true connection to what the psychic shared. So that even if she didn't believe in the woman, she believed she had been guided to hear what she had to say.

Like now.

The newest upload was also one in her pick-a-card.

And so, Bobbie did with curiosity. And then fast-forwarded the video to the section dedicated to all viewers who selected the second set of cards. And with each passing turn of the card and explanation of its meaning, Bobbie was again stunned by the accuracy as the woman spoke to heartbreak and conquering the fear of being hurt again.

"The fear is controlling you," the intuitive said. "Don't let it win. Forgiveness is your freedom."

Long after the video ended, those words clung more than any other.

Bobbie stood and grabbed her car fob from the corner of her desk before leaving her office, closing and locking the door behind her. The outer office was humming with activity as she strode past open doors, but her focus was on something else.

"Headed out?" Ms. Pott asked, following Bobbie's rapid movement toward the exit with her eyes over the rim of her glasses.

"Yes," Bobbie said over her shoulder.

"Where?"

"My past," Bobbie called as she turned and pressed her back and buttocks to the glass door to open it.

During the entire drive to the Weeksville section of Brooklyn, Bobbie regretted her rash decision. But she was trying to listen and follow her women's intuition. And it was screaming for closure. To move on and to heal.

Driving down the streets of Weeksville was nostalgic. She had once loved and cherished living in the notable area with such rich African American history, being founded by free African Americans. Named after

James Weeks, the African American owner of the land, the property went on to become a village complete with churches, schools, cemetery, newspaper and home for senior citizens. In time the history was forgotten by many until the late 1960s and the community was now officially preserved with four of the original homes designated landmarks.

She pulled to a stop on the street in front of the row of town houses. It was nothing near the grandeur of the Cress townhome, but she had loved the twelve-hundred-square-foot, two-story brick-faced house from the moment she first saw the home.

With foolish dreams of happily-ever-after.

Bobbie drummed her fingernails against the steering wheel as she eyed the mahogany wood front door with its wide beveled glass pane. She had chosen it wanting to give the home a warmer feel.

What am I doing?

In the divorce she had sold her share of the house to Henny and moved out, unable to stomach living where he had been bold enough to break their vows.

It's not for him. It's for you.

Bobbie climbed from her SUV and smoothed her hands over the cropped, off-shoulder sienna sweater she wore with distressed jeans. She came around the front to stand on the street with her fingers slid into her back pockets.

The fear is controlling you. Don't let it win. Forgiveness is your freedom.

With a nod to encourage herself, Bobbie crossed the sidewalk and walked up the stairs. She raised her hand to ring the doorbell with her free hand pressed to her bared belly. She felt nervous. It was undeniable.

"Bobbie?"

She turned to see her ex-husband, Henny Santana—still tall, dark and handsome with long black locks and a goatee—and standing on the street next to his mistress.

Bobbie's eyes dropped to the woman's belly swollen with pregnancy that looked near its end. "Oh," she said in understanding as pain pierced her like a hot blade.

She rushed down the stairs, leaving them both looking shocked and uncomfortable.

"Bobbie, esperar. Por favor," Henny called, following and reaching for her wrist as he pleaded for her to wait.

She snatched away from his touch and held up both hands, pleading with him not to test her grace. He hung his head as she focused her fury via her eyes on him.

"I didn't want you to find out like this," he said.

"How far along is your...your...your what?"

"Wife," he admitted. "And she's twenty-eight weeks."

Every bit of the destruction of his betrayal flooded her in waves until she felt weak and could only pray her legs did not give out beneath her as she came around the front of her car to open the driver's side door. She paused as the stabbing pain would not relent. "I regret the day I ever met you and every day after that until I got you out of my life. My bad for coming here and intruding on your new life. Let's pretend we never knew each other," she said, her tone bitter.

"Bobbie!" Henny called to her.

She ignored him and climbed into her car, hating the way her hands trembled as she started the ignition. She pulled away but only went two blocks before pulling into another parking spot. Old wounds were torn open. Raw and intense.

But she refused to cry and fought not to sink under the waves.

Of hurt. Disappointment. Bitterness.

"Rise, Bobbie. Rise," she encouraged herself as she pressed her hands together against her mouth. "Think higher. Be better. Do better. Help me, God."

It hurt. And there was no denying that. And deep amid that all too real and raw emotion she was finding it hard to cling to everything she had learned in her spiritual journey.

She swore and tilted her head back as the tears did rise and she released a low and jagged cry before a long breath. "Lying. Treacherous. Low-down. Disgusting. Piece of sh—"

Bzzzzzz. Bzzzzzz. Bzzzzzz.

She looked down through the blare of tears at her phone on the console. It read BIG BARNETT. She answered, putting it on Speaker. "Hey, Daddy," she said, fighting to sound like anything but her life in a shambles on a street in a neighborhood where she once lived.

"Something kept nagging at me to call. I had a fish on the line and everything," he said. "Everything okay? Is that the intuition you believe in?"

She sniffed. "I don't know what I believe because my gut instincts led me right into the middle of Henny's new life with his wife and a *baby* on the way," she said.

"Oh hell," Bobby sighed.

"I hate him. I do. I *hate* him with a passion. I hate him—"

"Don't let who he is change who you are, Bobbie. Be glad he is somebody else's problem," her father said.

She gazed out the window but focused on nothing. "I went to forgive him so I can move on and instead he's living the life I wanted with someone else. Like I never existed. Like I never mattered. Like I was filling her spot until he found *her*. Every time I brought up getting pregnant, he would put it off. *Not now*, he said. *I'm enjoying the two of us. Life is good.*"

"Bobbie, breathe, baby. I haven't heard you this upset in a long time," her father said.

Neither had she.

"Do you still love Henny? Is that what this is about?"

She shook her head before voicing it. "No. It's just feeling like he wasted my time because he knew—no matter how good he played the role of being happy— he knew I wasn't the one and so what I thought was an affair was more than that. Today, I saw it was more than that. He is *happy*. While I'm around here clutching crystals and being positive and finding the good and trying to heal and be better. And rise. All while living in *fear* of being hurt. He is happy. That pisses me off."

"You want him miserable?" Bobby asked.

"Yes!" she exclaimed, pounding her fist against the steering wheel. "I am."

"Are you, Bobbie? Are you truly miserable?" he asked, sounding like he didn't believe that.

She closed her eyes, and at that moment, she thought of Lincoln beside her atop the roller coaster encouraging her to be brave, open her eyes and enjoy the view. Her big, brooding, broad-shouldered British friend with the sarcastic mouth and hard stares had made her happy.

She pressed the back of her hand that he had kissed to her mouth. A smile came so easy. And somehow the joy carried her out of the darkness of pain. "No, I'm not miserable," she admitted softly.

Lincoln.

She envisioned him so clearly staring down at her as they stood outside The Met and he made her the offer for their charade. So tall and broad and handsome.

Her phone beeped with an incoming call and she peered at the line. She chuckled to see Lincoln Face-Time her. It was not the only time she would think of him and he would call.

"Thanks, Daddy. I'll call you back," she said, already reaching to answer Lincoln.

His handsome face filled the screen. She could see the bustle of his restaurant's kitchen in the background.

"Were you crying?" he asked.

"No," she lied as she noticed a dullness in his eyes and a grim set to his mouth—more than normal. "Lincoln, what's wrong?"

His eyes shifted away from the screen and with his profile, she could see he was clenching and unclenching his square jaw. He winced as he released several long breaths and shook his head a bit before dropping it.

"Lincoln. What's wrong?" she asked again with urgency as she clutched the phone.

He faced the screen again and the torment in his eyes cut her to the quick. "It's my mum. My mum just died," he said in a whisper. "My mum is gone."

She released a cry, hating the miles between them. Hating that she couldn't pull him close and comfort him. "Lincoln, I'm so sorry," she said. "I'm on the way. I will be there on the first damn thing headed that way. You hear me? I'm coming."

He nodded. "Please," he pleaded with no shame.

Barefoot with a glass of brandy in hand, Lincoln stood on the deck outside his master suite looking out at Carbis Bay Beach less than a thousand feet away. His glass one-story home was on a secluded enclave of the beach, offering him beauty, privacy and seclusion. The afternoon sun was high but there was still a nip in the air that he found invigorating. He needed to feel something besides the grief. It was constant.

He took a lingering sip of the drink and enjoyed the burn of it down his throat.

Not even the sands and turquoise waters offered any calm. And beneath the surface, he was fighting back anger. At himself. At the doctors. For a moment at God. And at his mother for not revealing her cancer diagnosis to him. For not taking treatment. Not fighting for her life.

"Damn," he swore, taking another sip.

One of many since he got the call the day before. One of many more to come.

He tipped his head back to drain the glass.

"Lincoln."

He lowered the glass and looked at Bobbie walking up the stone path pulling a roll-away suitcase behind her. The very sight of her was like water for thirst. He crossed the deck and came down the wooden steps to reach her. "You're here," he said, pulling her body into a tight embrace as she brought her hands up his back.

Even through the woven cotton of the white shirt he wore, he felt goose bumps race across his body at her closeness.

"You're barefoot," she teased.

"I'm *home*," he stressed. "How was your trip?"

"I flew private," she said, looking up at him with her chin settled against the groove between his biceps.

"And then hired a car service to drive me here. So yes. I am here. And how are you?"

Lincoln looked down into her face, with her bright eyes filled with concern for him and her mouth as tempting as ever. The desire to kiss her filled him as the wind blew her wild hair and the smell of the sea blended with the scent of her honey. It felt good to have her close. In his arms. And his life.

"Thank you for coming, Bobbie," he said, refraining from tasting her mouth as he respected the limits set by their friendship.

His grief needed that more than their attraction.

Lincoln pressed a kiss to her forehead before letting her go and taking the handle of her suitcase to pick it up. "Are you hungry?" he asked, looking down at her profile.

"Starving," she said. "How about you? Have you had anything but bourbon?"

"Ever the detective," he teased with a shake of his head as they climbed the stairs up to the deck. "You miss nothing."

She just wrapped her arms around one of his and leaned her head against it as he slid open the glass door and offered her to enter first. When she released him to do so, he missed their connection.

"Lincoln, your home is beautiful," she said, turning in the center of the living room to take in the small well-appointed but thousand-square-foot one-bedroom beach house. It was an abundance of windows and teak wood with modern furniture in latte with chocolate leather accents. Black dome-shaped pendant lights of varying lengths offered warmth. A freestanding bubble-shaped metal fireplace floated from the wood-planked ceiling serving as art as well as function.

"Thank you," he said, eyeing the place and how he could view the sand and water with little to no intrusion. "My mother hired a designer when I first purchased it. I was so upset with her but she was right. It's exactly what I didn't know I needed."

Bobbie turned to look at him. "Let's talk about your mum," she said with a soft smile.

Lincoln scratched his goatee and shook his head. "Not ready yet. You know?" he said, his voice low and his eyes pained.

She nodded as she came over to stand beside him. "Okay. I have to find a hotel but I will always be just a call away," she promised.

"A hotel?" he balked. "You'll stay here."

A look he couldn't quite identify filled her face before she gave him a hesitant smile and soft shake of her head. "No, Lincoln. No," she said.

He walked away from her with her suitcase in hand. "It's a one-bedroom but I'll sleep on the sofa," he said, glancing back over his shoulder as he continued to a closed bedroom door.

"*No*, Lincoln," Bobbie stressed coming around his body to stand in his path and block him from proceeding forward. "No."

He set the suitcase down in the hall and settled his hand low on his hips. "You're welcome here…with me, Bobbie," he said, locking eyes with hers. "I want you here…with me."

Bobbie glanced down, interrupting the stare.

He wiggled his toes.

She looked up at him with a smile that soon faded.

"We didn't do so well with close quarters at the hotel. Remember?"

"Remember?" he asked with a yawn as he stretched his arms high above his head. "I can't forget...*but* the last thing on my mind is sex right now."

"Right," she agreed, diverting her eyes away from the rigid definition of his abdomen.

Lincoln did not miss it as he lowered his arms. "Hey," he called to her softly.

"Somehow—and I don't get it any more than you— but you have become my best friend," he said. "Stay. Please."

She nodded and tucked her hair behind her ear. "Whatever you want."

Lincoln arched a brow.

"I—I—I meant. Whatever you need."

He cleared his throat and shook his head. "Try again," he said, enjoying a moment of levity from his grief as he teased her.

She grabbed her suitcase and stepped inside the bedroom. "I'm going to shower and change and then we'll *both* grab something to eat," she said. "No more alcohol."

He shrugged both shoulders and splayed his fingers before turning to walk back down the hall. In the kitchen he went to the bar station he kept on the corner of the thick glass countertop tinted the same aquamarine as the sea. He grabbed the bottle of aged bourbon and another glass as he made his way back to the deck to fold his body into the weathered leather sling seat of the lone deck chair. He poured himself three fingers of the alcohol and finished it in two swallows as he looked out at the cloud-filled blue skies become the deep blues of the sea in the distance. Because of the wind, he could smell the sea and see the white caps of the waves.

Setting the bottle and glass on the deck beside the chair, Lincoln stretched his legs and crossed his feet at the ankles. Closing his eyes, he envisioned his mother smiling at him as she ran barefoot along the sand. Living and loving life without a care in the world.

Pain crippled his chest at that coming to an end.

And when alcohol-fueled sleep offered reprieve from his sorrow, Lincoln was unable to fight it.

He blinked several times as he awakened, surprised by the darkness and the moon blazing like an orb in the sky.

"Welcome back."

His eyes shot to the sound of Bobbie's husky voice to find her sitting on the long cushions lining the edge of the deck. He was startled. As if she was yet another of the dreams he had where memories of her lovemaking taunted him. "How long have I been asleep?" he asked.

"Ten hours," she said, dressed in a long-sleeved cropped white pullover and matching yoga pants, her hair in a tousled topknot with several loose strands and fuzzy slippers on her feet.

With the starry sky as her backdrop and the crackle of the outdoor fireplace now lit, she looked in her element.

And adorable.

"My apologies," he said, looking to find his bottle of liquor gone. "I'm not much of a host."

"I'm not here for you to entertain me," she said. "I'm a grown woman. I took a nap. Walked the beach. Handled some business calls."

"Hungry?" he asked for the second time that day.

Bobbie stood up. "I cooked," she said, raising crossed fingers.

He averted his eyes away from the sight of her hips and thighs in the clinging pants she wore. "Really?" he asked. "Uhm. *Can* you cook?"

"Just wait and see," she said, walking inside the house.

Lincoln pulled back the throw Bobbie must have settled over him to rise and stoke the fire. He enjoyed the warmth and the smell of the cherry wood. As he rose to his full height, he looked through the glass at Bobbie moving about his kitchen.

When he got the news, she was the first person he thought of calling and now here she was without hesitation. She flew across the ocean to help him through a difficult time. And she fit like a puzzle piece.

He had to force his eyes away from her as she headed back across the house with his large leather tray in her hands. He moved to open the door for her.

"Thanks," she said.

Lincoln followed her over to the deck cushions surprised to find his appetite had returned. "What did you make?" he asked as they sat down with the tray between them.

"Fish," she said, handing him a plate and cutlery.

Lincoln studied the crusted monkfish stuffed with lobster, spinach and lobster mushroom atop thinly sliced potatoes baked in lemon, garlic, butter and rosemary. "You cooked this?" he asked, as he cut the tender fish with his fork to slide into his mouth.

"Absolutely not," Bobbie said with a chuckle. "My culinary skills go as far as scrambling eggs and ordering from DoorDash. Your sous chef sent several dishes from your restaurant for you."

Lincoln took a moment to savor the fish that tasted similar to lobster. "Considering it's one of the first dishes I created for the menu at SHORES when we opened. Yes, I know," he said with an amused look.

"It's delicious, Lincoln," she said, doing a little dance as she chewed.

He fell silent and looked out into the moon's light cast down upon the water. "It was the only thing my mum ordered at SHORES. Sometimes every night," he said.

At the feel of Bobbie's hand on his, he looked at her.

"Talk to me about her, Lincoln," she encouraged him.

"She wasn't perfect, but she was the perfect mother for me," he admitted, maybe for the first time to himself or anyone else. "And she loved and lived life to the fullest. With no hesitation. Didn't give a damn what anyone thought. And I hate that it used to frustrate me because now that's she's gone—*way* too soon—I now know she deserved to live how she wanted. To enjoy every moment."

Bobbie's grip on his hand tightened.

"She would cheer for me louder than anyone else in the room—and it didn't matter where we were. School. Church. The grocery store. The pub. My restaurant," Lincoln said as his chest tightened with sorrow as he pictured his mother so clearly. "She would cup her hands around her mouth and let out a holler. And then raise both arms high in the air and clap like a seal while she yelled out *That's* my *kid*!"

"Oh, Lincoln," Bobbie sighed.

He hung his head to block her from seeing the tears

that welled. "I will never hear that again," he said with a shake of his head.

Bobbie rose to stand behind him with her chin atop his head, to hold him from behind and give the comfort he needed as he gave in to his grief and mourned his mother as tears racked his body.

"I'm here," she said softly in between pressing kisses to his head. "I'm here. Let it out. I got you."

And Lincoln believed that without a doubt.

Seven

Bobbie stared across the beach house at Lincoln glancing through the pages of a photo album he brought back from his mother's apartment above the SHORES. They had spent the day packing up her things, giving a good bit of the clothing to friends of hers in need. She poured herself another glass of the red wine he opened and reclaimed her seat on the sofa next to Lincoln.

She took a sip and looked down at a photo he held in his hand. Even as a child he had the most serious expression. Bobbie nudged her shoulder against his arm. "Have you ever smiled, Lincoln?" she asked.

He shrugged one shoulder. "Lord knows my mother tried," he said. "This was at the fair—believe it or not. I was six and ready to go home. And never went back again."

"So that's why you never rode an amusement park

ride before," Bobbie said, thinking of his insistence on riding the roller coaster with her that day on the Jersey Shore.

"Exactly," he admitted, replacing the photo in the album to remove another. "She would nag me to have children so that she could see how it felt to go to the amusement with a fun kid."

Bobbie eyed his profile as he stared down at a photo of his mother in her early twenties with a bikini top, jean cutoffs and roller skates. "A mini Lincoln with a scowl is adorable *to me*," she said.

"One day," he responded, closing the album to sit on the small round coffee table. "What about you? Are children a part of your plan?"

Bobbie looked away. Instantly thinking of Henny's new life and being pained by it. Those raw emotions she felt just before Lincoln's call about his mother's death were still there waiting their turn to take dominance.

"What's going on?" Lincoln asked. "I'm sorry if I was intrusive."

Bobbie shook her head and turned her face to lock eyes with him. "No, it's not you," she said wanting to reassure him. "I found my ex has remarried and has a baby on the way—which would be just fine *if* he hadn't put me off about having children for years."

Quickly she told him about her visit to the home she once shared with her husband and her shocking discovery.

"He's a damn fool," Lincoln stressed.

Bobbie ran her free hand through her waves with a light laugh. "Isn't he?" she agreed.

"Hey," Lincoln said softly.

Bobbie was now used to him doing that to get her attention. "Yes, Lincoln," she said, settling back against the couch and kicking off her shoes to tuck her feet beneath her bottom.

"Can I give you some advice that you once gave me?" Lincoln asked.

"Do I want to hear this?" she asked before taking another sip of her wine.

"Probably not."

She forced a smile.

Lincoln turned his body on the sofa to face her. "What if you weren't meant to have a kid for this man who didn't honor or respect you? What if what was meant to be was you falling in love with the right guy and *then* having a baby—a beautiful baby girl with doe eyes, wild hair and a big mouth."

As he said each his eyes touched on her same features.

Her eyes.

Her hair.

Her mouth.

She bit down onto it.

His eyes dropped to take in the move, but then he shook himself as if to deny the attraction. "So," he continued, running his hand over his mouth. "What if he just got out of your way for the future you're meant to have with someone else? Change your way of looking at it."

Bobbie let her head fall back and chuckled. "So *now* you believe in fate and destiny and all of that?" she asked. *"Really?"*

"Hey."

She faced him. "What if. Right?"

He held up his hands. "What if?" he said. "That's all I'm saying."

Enlightened Lincoln is annoying...and right.

Bobbie raised her glass to him in a toast before giving him a reluctant smile.

Hours later, Lincoln leaned in the door frame, nursing a snifter of scotch and soda as he watched Bobbie on the beach meditating. He looked up at the full pink supermoon in the sky. He had to admit that it did appear bigger and brighter than normal full moons like she said it would. She explained that the moon was a rare occurrence and held spiritual significance for its abilities to heal emotional difficulties.

Lincoln was a skeptic through and through, but he sat back quietly as she journaled about her dreams and manifestations. And he adored her show of joy and exuberance as she raced barefoot out to the beach at 11:33 p.m. when the supermoon was biggest and brightest to meditate and absorb all of its good energy.

Although he knew the moon only appeared pink, he had to admit it was quite a sight against the dark skies and above tranquil water. The ideal scenic landscape.

He was tempted to just sit beside her but didn't want to intrude. She looked so peaceful and relaxed. But when she jumped to her feet and went running full speed to jump into the water, Lincoln pushed aside his shock and set his drink down to go racing across the deck and then the beach to join her.

Bobbie tightened the towel wrapped around her damp hair as she sat at the island watching Lincoln cook them dinner at nearly two in the morning. She covered her mouth as a yawn escaped. "We need to get some sleep," she said as he opened the oven to remove a sheet pan of thick and crispy pork belly. "The funeral is pretty early in the morning."

Lincoln cut his eyes up at her as he removed the pork onto the cutting board and used a butcher knife to turn them into chunks. "I still can't believe she planned it herself," he said, turning to stir the large pot with its contents bubbling away on the stove. "I had nothing to do but pay the bill and show up."

"I think every decision she made was to lighten the load for you," she said, knowing his frustration with his mother not disclosing her declining health. "A mother 'til the very end."

Bobbie paused at his intensity as he rapidly sliced fresh herbs to dash into the pot. It was the same look he wore during sex—focused and determined to deliver his *very* best.

And he did just that.

Memories of that night came back. Stroke after stroke after stroke.

She released a low and brief whistle as she shifted in her seat while her desire for him caused her bud to awaken with throbs.

Just friends.

Lincoln glanced up at the sun brightly glowing in the sky and had to wince because of its brilliance. The weather was even warmer than normal with a comforting spring breeze. It was just the type of day his mother would want for her last hurrah.

That and red sequin pumps with her ankles crossed in the coffin like the Queen of Soul Aretha Franklin's had been.

As the coffin was lowered into the ground, Lincoln reached for Bobbie's hand and was comforted when she instantly gripped his with her own. She would be returning to her life soon and he didn't know if his home would ever be the same without her in it.

"Ladies and gentlemen, Poppy had one final request."

Lincoln looked at the funeral director holding a laptop. The tall and thin man gave him a comforting smile as he opened the computer. His mother's smiling face appeared on the screen and waved—with her lashes, red lipstick and long nails in place.

An ache of missing her radiated across his chest.

"Hi there, everyone. Don't be cross with me because I didn't tell you that the last you saw me was the *very* last time you would see me," she began with a wistful look in her eyes. "Like I've done my whole life I went out having fun, laughing and making other people laugh. Right?"

Nearly the entire town of St. Ives was in attendance and there was a swell of agreement.

"Lincoln. I know you, *my* son. You're troubled that I didn't give you a chance to take me to every doctor and spend every bit of your hard-earned money trying to stop the inevitable. My brilliant, talented, stubborn, *grouchy* son with a good heart, I need you to forgive your mum," she said softly, dropping her head for a moment before facing them once again with tears in her eyes.

Bobbie tightened her grip on his hand.

"You're the best thing I ever did, kid. You were so good to your mum. *So* good," she stressed, clasping her hands together. "You never once complained about my pub tab. Never *once*. And plenty of you in the crowd benefitted."

Chuckles floated up from the throng.

Poppy released a heavy breath, just like Lincoln would do so often. "Lincoln, I love you more than a million words could tell ya. Here's some advice from your mum. *Live* life, son. Have more fun. Laugh a little. Fall in love. Have babies. For God's sake find a reason to smile. Life is sometimes short and all I want for my kid is no regrets."

Lincoln nodded as if she could see him.

"And for the crowd—my friends—when you see my boy and he's looking a little down for missing his mum, do me favor?" she asked, with a wimpy smile. "Raise your hands way up in the air like this and clap like this and tell him that he is and will always be Poppy's kid."

With one last wink, the video faded to black.

And that broke him—seeing her one last time with her arms high in the air as her claps echoed into the wind and she cheered for him. Loudly and with boldness. Like always.

He hung his head so very low.

Bobbie rested her head against his arm.

And then he felt hands—one by one—land against his shoulders and back. He looked back to find his brothers had come forward from the crowd to surround him. Support him.

Phillip Junior. Sean. Gabriel. Coleman. And Lucas.

He needed them more than ever.

* * *

Bobbie smiled at the crowd surrounding Phillip Senior at the pub as his hometown residents enjoyed his return. It was the first time Bobbie had seen the stalwart man laughing and not stiff and foreboding. Nicolette stood close by with a soft smile as she observed her husband in a bit of surprise as if she had never seen him that relaxed either.

But then Bobbie remembered Lincoln telling her that the woman accused her of selling gossip on the Cress family to the tabloids. She had to fight the temptation to confront the woman and get her straight, but she didn't want to be the one to cause a wedge between Lincoln and his family.

Especially now. Wrong time. Wrong place.

Nicolette looked over at her and Bobbie did not shift her gaze away from her. With an arch of her brow, she raised her flute of champagne to the older woman in an unspoken promise.

One day soon.

Shifting her gaze, she found Lincoln at the bar surrounded by his brothers. All tall and broad shouldered and handsome, but it was Lincoln upon which her look lingered and she allowed herself to drop the invisible wall she had put up between herself and her desire for him to just enjoy the beauty of him. Every bit.

Lincoln made brooding so damn sexy.

And although he didn't show it, she knew he was surprised and pleased at the appearance of his entire Cress family at the funeral for his mother. They arrived that morning and were scheduled to leave that same night. But they were there for him.

She had come to learn that like many families, the Cress family was flawed but there was love. Plenty of it. And Lincoln needed it now more than ever.

"They make quite a sight. Don't they?" Monica asked, tracing her fingertip around the edge of her glass of champagne with her head tilted slightly to the side as she eyed Gabriel.

Bobbie spied the promise of naughty frivolities in the woman's eyes. As she looked around the table where they sat there was that same light in the eyes of Jillian and Raquel. But she got it. She understood it completely because that one night with Lincoln had her just as hooked and hungry for more.

"Bobbie?"

She turned and had to tilt her head up to see the face of a tall and curvaceous woman with straight hair, a medium brown complexion and a hint of something Bobbie couldn't identify in her eyes. "Yes?" she asked.

"I'm Raven. Lincoln's...friend," the woman said with emphasis, extending her hand.

Bobbie gave her a smile as smooth as softened butter and shook her offered hand. "Nice to meet you," she said, inspecting Lincoln's ex.

During one of their all-night talkfests during her stay in St. Ives, he had revealed Raven's reluctance to end their no-strings relationship.

The woman said nothing but remained standing there. Bobbie furrowed her brows a bit. "Is there something I can help you with?" she asked, not hiding her confusion or building annoyance.

Raven gave her a smile and a shake of her head before walking away with one last glance back over her shoulder before leaving the pub.

"What in the hell was that about?" Jillian asked.

"Someone hooked on the Cress family jewel," Bobbie drawled.

The women all laughed.

"If y'all getting it as good as I am, then we're all blessed," Raquel said with a flirty raise of her arched eyebrows as she took a sip from her flute.

"Phillip Junior?" the three women said in unison.

Raquel laughed. "Listen. I don't put up with his blind ambition for nothing," she assured them.

Bobbie turned and found Lincoln looking at her with concern. She gave him a smile to ease any worries but he excused himself and strode across the crowded pub to reach her side, bending down beside her.

"What's wrong?" he asked.

"Nothing. Your ex just made her introductions," she said with a wicked chuckle.

"She's not my ex. We were never together," he said.

Bobbie laughed. "Oh, I'm sure you two were *together*," she teased, reaching up to loosen the knot of the black tie he wore before patting his chest with her palm.

His face became tight. "You know what I mean," he drawled.

"If she's not your ex, then *what* is she?"

"A mistake I wish I never made," he muttered before rising to turn and walk back over to his brothers.

Lincoln slowly turned in a circle in the flat above his restaurant. It was here in the small two-bedroom place where he had been raised for a good chunk of his life. Just him and Poppy. When he purchased the pub where she once worked and renovated it to a restaurant, she had been so proud. And when he handed her the keys to the refurbished apartment she had cried, danced and laughed endlessly while she hugged him.

She's really gone.

"Son."

Lincoln turned to find his father standing in the open doorway. After the postfuneral pub gathering to celebrate the life of his mother, which was traditional in England, Lincoln had invited his family to the restaurant for a private dinner before their flight back to the states. He had felt proud of their praise of his design and menu.

They were the best of the best in the culinary world after all.

For a moment, he felt defensive knowing his mother would not want him there.

"I'm not coming in," Phillip Senior said, holding up hands that unmistakably belonged to a longtime chef—calloused, marked by years of chopping with a knife and scarred by occasional cuts. "I've been made *very* aware of just how Poppy felt about me."

Bloody wanker.

One of his mother's many insults about the man floated from his memory easily.

"But there has been a misunderstanding all these years," Phillip Senior said.

"About?" Lincoln asked.

"I was talking to one of Poppy's friends at the pub. It seems your mother wrote a letter telling me she was pregnant when she was three months or so," his father began, leaning in the doorway. "But by then I had already left for Paris a month before and my parents no longer lived in St. Ives, having sold the farm where I grew up. That's all confirmable. I never got the letter, Lincoln."

Lincoln looked at his father.

"I never would knowingly abandon a child of mine. *Never*," he swore with a steady gaze.

Lincoln gave him a nod, accepting his words as truth.

"I am proud to call you my son," Phillip Senior said. "We have much more to talk about. But not tonight."

"No," Lincoln said, looking around his mother's apartment and feeling her absence. "Not tonight."

Bobbie checked the time on her laptop where she had been reviewing the monthly reports to sign off for electronic payments to be processed to her large roster of private investigators. It was nearly midnight but only near seven in New York. She called Ms. Pott via FaceTime. Soon her face filled the screen.

"Hello, stranger," she said.

Bobbie smiled at her. "It's only been a week," she said, picking up the cup of tea she had prepared for herself.

"How's the Brit?" Ms. Pott asked with concern.

"The funeral was yesterday," Bobbie said, glancing at the open bedroom door. "Earlier today when he was dozing off, I insisted he take a nap stretched out across the bed while I worked. That was more than eight hours ago. I think there was nothing more he could do but sleep."

"Sleep restores and heals. Let him be," Ms. Pott said.

Bobbie nodded in agreement.

"You ready to leave him?"

No.

But Bobbie protected that truth because it was something she wasn't ready to accept. "I need to get home and get back to my cases. Get back to work," was all that she offered.

"Well, your flight is in the morning. You're all booked. First-class."

"See you soon, Ms. Pott," Bobbie said before ending the call.

She took a deep sip of her sweet tea as she rose to move down the hall to the bedroom to peek in on Lincoln. One thin strip of moonlight broke free of the curtains to offer enough illumination to see he lay in the middle of the bed with his arms beneath his head. It was all so cliché, but as she looked down at him, she enjoyed his handsome face not lined with frowns. In sleep, he was adorable.

Feeling moved to do so, she bent over and pressed an air kiss to his brow.

"I'm not sleeping."

His voice startled her and her heart reacted as she looked down into his eyes now open and piercing her. She began to rise and he brought his hand up to lightly cup the back of her neck to keep her secured in place. Just inches above him. Their eyes locked. Inhaling each other's breath. Charging that energy that always pulsed between them. Taken with each other.

By moonlight.

"Bobbie," he said with hunger as his eyes dipped to her mouth in that tiny second before he raised his head to capture it with his own.

As his tongue traced her lip, she dropped the mug and barely felt the cooled liquid splash against her leg as he jerked her body down atop his and then rolled their bodies until he was atop her, pressing her into the bed.

The moan she released was bursting with her pleasure at the feel of him gently sucking the tip of her tongue as he eased his strong hands down the sides of her body to cup her buttocks. She dug her fingers into his shoulders as she brought one leg up to wrap around his waist. "Lincoln," she gasped into his mouth.

It was good. And all too familiar.

She thought of that night on the floor of the hotel. And her regrets. Her stance to not break her one-year rule again.

But here we are...

She broke their kiss. "What *are* we doing?" she asked.

"Giving in," he said, his heated eyes searching her face.

"Again," she stressed. "I can't. We can't. For what? We did the same thing in New York and you left the next day. I leave in the morning. Why now? No flings, remember?"

Lincoln pressed a kiss between her brows that made her shiver. And then another to her cheeks and then her chin. "I want you. And I am tired of finding reasons not to want you, Bobbie," he admitted.

"Lincoln—"

"Why are we fighting this attraction that is not going away?" he asked. "You are so damn sexy to me that even watching you brush your teeth excites me. I am distracted by thoughts of you all day and then I dream of you at night. Having you. I am always thinking about you. About us."

Us.

That sounds good.

"What about us?" she asked, feeling nervous and afraid because hope sprang to life in her chest.

"I don't want a fling. I want more than sex. I want you out of my head and into my life," he said in between kisses to her mouth. "We can do this. We *have* been doing this."

Bobbie closed her eyes and turned her head to break the magic of his kisses, but he just pressed his lips to the length of her throat making her squirm. The length of his hardness pressed against her core. It distracted her from her reasonings.

Made her forget her one-year plan.

Again.

Made her want to forget it forever.

Lincoln. Lincoln. Lincoln.

She yearned for him. Ached for him. Wanted him. It would not let up. "Yes, Lincoln," she sighed.

And when he shifted his body down to raise her T-shirt and sports bra above her breasts, she arched her back as he captured one taut nipple in his mouth. Her gasp of pleasure echoed around them. It was matched with another as he lightly flickered his tongue against the other. Endlessly.

She was trembling, hot and wet for him.

And when he cut his eyes up to look at her, she saw the same hunger she felt, but there was something else amid their passion and desire.

As he rose to his knees on the bed to slowly undress her with caresses and kisses with each reveal of her body, she felt such a profound connection to him. Her eyes were glued to his body, feasting on his beauty as he tugged his T-shirt over his head to fling it away and then worked the sweatpants and boxer shorts he wore around the long length of his aroused inches. His body was like steel—hard and unrelenting. Built to last. And his inches were thick as they hung away from his body surrounded by a thick patch of dark curly hair. The tip of him was smooth and built for entry.

But she wasn't quite ready for that. And neither was Lincoln as he took his time to explore and enjoy her body. Relish it. Praise it. Kiss and caress it. All of her. From her shoulders to her cleavage and then each peak of her breasts. Her belly. Her hips. Even her knees before he spread them and lowered his head to feast on her. Slowly though.

It was sweet torture and Bobbie felt light-headed from the euphoria.

"The best. You are the best," she whispered with her back arched and her hands pressed to the back of his head as she gently thrust her hips back and forth as he devoured her intimacy bringing her to a slow climax.

Her cries filled the air. High-pitched screams and whimpers in her throat took turns as he suckled her bud with ravenous moans that only pushed her further over the edge. She didn't know whether to shove him away or pull him closer. Just sheer madness.

She loved it.

Lincoln rose to look down at her in wonder as he licked the taste of her from his lips. "Look at you," he moaned, before leaning over to remove a condom from the nightstand.

Still trembling and weak, Bobbie sat up and locked her mouth on one of his flat nipples as she took the protection from him to hold in one hand and wrapped the other around his inches. It was hot and so hard. She felt his body tremor. It fueled her. She wanted to please him and to see the power she held to entice him. To know that they were captured in this world of crazy passion together. Equals. Pleasing and being pleased.

With heated eyes, she lowered her head.

At the first feel of her tasting him, Lincoln thrust his hips forward and released a roar that seemed torn from his belly as he wove his fingers in her hair to lightly grip. "No," he cried, freeing his inches. "I was about to explode."

Her smile was wicked as she wiped the corners of her mouth with her finger before opening the condom and rolling it down on his inches with both her hands.

With a shake of his head, Lincoln pressed her body back down onto the bed and kissed her deeply as he guided his thick tip to her core. Every muscle in his body was cut and defined as he controlled entering her slowly. With ease. Spreading her. Filling her until the root of him was planted inside her.

At her wince, Lincoln raised his head to study her face. "You okay?" he asked.

"I just *feel* you," she whispered before she bit her bottom lip. "All of you. *Whoo*. It's—it's impressive."

Lincoln's smile came slowly but fully, revealing twin dimples.

Bobbie's eyes widened in shock. "I knew I would make you smile," she teased softly, massaging him from his strong back to his buttocks. "You should do it more often—you're beautiful with it."

"Oh yeah?" he asked as he began to stroke inside her.

She grunted from the wicked feel of him as she answered him with a nod. "Lincoln," she whispered, lost in his eyes and hungry for his mouth as he made love to her slowly. So sensual. So passion-driven.

Electricity sparked between them.

Bobbie brought her hands up to massage his shoulders before she pressed her palms to his face and tilted her head to the side to look at him in marvel. She bent her legs and pressed her feet into the bed as she circled her hips in unison with his.

He pursed his lips. "Yes," he moaned. "Yes."

It was her turn to smile.

Noticing that, he picked up the pace and deepened his strokes.

Her smile was replaced with a deep bite of her bottom lip.

"The thought of you leaving tomorrow made me realize that I need you in my life, Bobbie Barnett," he said, pausing in his strokes. "Tell me we can figure this out."

Her fear—and old hurt—was there with all the naysaying.

It's too soon.

It's long distance.

What if doesn't work?

What if he hurts you?

The fear is controlling you. Don't let it win. Forgiveness is your freedom.

Over the days, as Bobbie had stayed with Lincoln and helped him prepare and then attend his mother's funeral, they had moved with the energy of a couple. She had liked the feel and idea of that.

It felt right. More right than any other relationship.

Trust my gut.

She gave him a hesitant smile and nodded before raising her head to kiss him even as her fear fought to reign over her desire. Passion won and nothing else mattered. Time was lost as they rode the waves of pleasure together until their bodies were damp with their sweat, hearts pounded and soon their mingled cries filled the air as they furiously worked for that white-hot explosion that left them both breathless and spent.

Eight

One month later

Bobbie was bursting with anticipation.

She could barely maintain focus on the meeting with Monica, Gabe's fiancée, and her team for her nonprofit, The Bridge. After years of being raised in the turbulent foster care system, Monica wanted to provide crucial financial help to those foster care kids who turned eighteen and "aged out" of the system with no resources to start their adult life.

Bobbie remembered the salacious scandal of the former housekeeper of the Cress family discovering her father was an A-list movie star, Brock Maynard, who had given her up but then left her his entire fortune upon his death last year. She loved that the woman was using her newfound wealth to help others in need.

From the head of the conference table in her offices, Bobbie watched the trio of women gathered there. Along with Monica, there was Choice Kingsley, a prominent attorney serving as the nonprofit's legal counsel, and Montgomery Morgan, a sought-after publicist.

"We think connecting with a private investigative firm to locate the kids who aged out of the system and seemed to have disappeared is an important part of the problem that we're missing," Monica explained.

Bobbie eyed the woman and understood why Gabe was unabashedly in love with her. Monica was beautiful, smart, compassionate and generous. She liked her and her gut instinct told her to trust her.

"They may need the help of The Bridge more than anyone," Choice added.

"And this partnership could also be advantageous for B. Barnett Investigations," Montgomery chimed in with a smooth and polished smile.

"*Or* it could just be the right thing to do," Bobbie said, eyeing the polished and poised woman with a caramel complexion, long hair, and narrow eyes with lush lashes that gave a smoldering look. "See, a better sell for me would be helping find kids who may be homeless, or hurt or worse get connected with help. And that doesn't require press. No offense."

"Yes, but garnering recognition for the foundation leads to more donations which leads to more ability to help," Montgomery said politely. "It's *all* full circle and necessary. No offense."

She takes no mess. But like Lincoln, she could use some really good sex. Her entire posture is tense. Nothing like a good climax—or two—to relax those shoulders and back.

Bobbie released the urge to say that.

"The Bridge is very important to me," Monica stressed.

"So much so that you haven't taken the time to plan a wedding," Choice chided her playfully. "How in the world are Cole and Jillian getting married before you and Gabe?"

Monica massaged the bridge of her nose. "You sound like Gabe," she said. "He wants something small. Just family and a few friends."

Bobbie noted the time on her phone, feeling the convo had turned decidedly more pleasure than business. Normally she would indulge, but she had other plans. She cleared her throat. "Good luck with the wedding plans," she began with a smile. "And I'm in on the collaboration."

"You'll work with The Bridge?" Monica asked.

After acquiring her massive inheritance and discovering her paternity, it was Monica who hired Bobbie to locate her mother. It had been difficult to inform her of her death. But then Monica recommended her to Gabe and Cole when they wanted their father investigated.

"We seem to do a lot of business together," Bobbie said, picking up her phone to watch the time.

"If it's not broken why fix it?" Monica said with a warm smile, even as her eyes dipped to take in the move. "You have plans?"

The door to the office opened and Lincoln stepped inside, looking so handsome in a navy-crisp gray button-up shirt and dark denims, wearing a smile as his eyes locked on her.

"Yes," Bobbie said, breathless as she rose to her feet.

It had been a month since they'd seen each other. And that was far too long. "Him."

Lincoln was in America for Cole and Jillian's wedding that weekend.

Monica looked toward the entrance and her eyes widened in surprise. "Lincoln! And he's *smiling*?" she said. "I've never seen him smile before."

Bobbie glanced down at her with a wink. "I give him plenty to smile about," she said.

"Nice," Choice said, studying him. "Good for you."

Bobbie chuckled. "Yes. Monica, let's talk soon and figure out the details," she said as she watched Lincoln talk to her inquisitive office manager even as he kept his intense stare locked on her.

The women rose to their feet on their high heels.

Bobbie led the way across the space, trying her very best not to run to him. And as soon as she reached him, Lincoln slid a strong arm around her waist and picked her up with ease to capture her mouth with his own. She released a moan as his tongue circled hers and he tasted of it with hunger.

"Hi, Lincoln. *Bye*, Lincoln," Monica drawled teasingly as she passed on her way out the door.

Bobbie tilted her head back to break the kiss. "Welcome back," she sighed, rubbing the brown-tinted gloss from his lips with her thumb.

"Glad to be back," he said.

"Get a room," Ms. Pott chirped in from behind them.

Lincoln glanced back over his shoulder and gave her a teasing look. "Gladly. Hold all calls, please," he quipped, before letting Bobbie down to her feet.

She took his hand and led him toward her office to use her entrance to her loft.

"I don't work for you," Ms. Pott called behind them.

Bobbie stopped and looked back. "Then hold all calls for me," she said.

Ms. Pott's eyes twinkled. "Gladly," she said.

Lincoln lay on his side and looked down at Bobbie as she slept. Darkness reigned but pockets of night-lights lined the brick walls and offered enough illumination for him to enjoy the sight of her. Her mouth was slightly opened and her face relaxed as she released a low—but unmistakable—snore.

She deserved the slumber.

They'd barely left the bed since his arrival. Only when necessary. Just to return to it for more.

More kisses.

More touches.

More strokes.

And even now as he watched her sleep with the sheet down around her waist as she lay on her back, he wanted even more. And not just hot and explosive sex.

More smiles.

More laughs.

More talks.

More plans for the future.

During the last month, stepping fully into having Bobbie as his woman had more joy and peace than he'd ever known.

He nuzzled his face into her wild hair and enjoyed the fresh smell of something fruity as he pressed a kiss to her scalp. With one swift move, he grabbed the sheet to fling back from their bodies, exposing their nudity and his stirring erection. "Bobbie," he whispered, pressing light kisses to her mouth as he glided his hand across the ample and clean-shaven mound of her core to open her plump lips.

Bobbie released a soft grunt of pleasure as he teased the fleshy bud hidden there. It swelled with life and pulsed against his fingers, matching the increased pace of his heartbeat.

"Bobbie. Come on, baby. Wake up," he whispered against her lips as he slid one and then another finger inside her tight core, feeling resistance to any more.

She gasped and arched her back as she spread her legs wider—nearly into a split.

"Is it the yoga that has you so flexible?"

"Yes," she gasped in between deep breaths of air.

"Damn," he stressed.

His inches lengthened with hardness. He ached for her. Loved the look of rapture on her face as she bit her bottom lip and winced, reaching to grip his hardness. To stroke. From root to tip.

Lincoln shivered and pressed his hips forward into her hand, weakened by her touch.

Bobbie opened her eyes to look up at him as she tilted her face up and offered him the tip of her tongue. He circled her pulsing bud and kissed her deeply as if drawing life from her. He swallowed her cries of pleasure as he brought her to an explosive climax that caused the walls of her intimacy to grip and release the fingers planted inside her with each riotous wave.

Watching her in the throes of release as her moist heat dampened his fingers, plus the quickened pace of her hand on him brought on his explosion. Fast and furious. He released a wild cry with his mouth open, and his heart pounded as he climaxed. And she did not relent until he was spent, shivering and coated in sweat as he waited for his body to be of his possession again.

Bobbie watched Lincoln across the same table in the Midtown Manhattan restaurant where they had their first contentious meeting. "We've come a long way," she said, flipping her hair back over her shoulder as she traced the edge of her wineglass with her fingertip.

Lincoln looked up from the menu he had been studying with a chuckle. "You're remembering that night too?" he asked.

She nodded.

"Whatever happened with that couple?"

"They're still together, believe it or not."

Lincoln's brows went up in shock. "Good luck to them," he said, raising his snifter of brandy.

"I second that," Bobbie agreed. "People change. Look at us. From aggravating each other's nerves to—"

Needing you.

Lincoln's eyes filled with warmth. "To?" he asked with the hint of a smile at her pause.

The fear of hurt and betrayal that she constantly battled rose. *When will this be easy?* she thought.

He makes me want it to be easy.

"Needing you," she finally finished, setting aside fear and claiming her happiness with him.

Lincoln rose and came around the small round table to stoop down beside her. She met his look as he pressed his palm to the side of her face and stroked her jawline with his calloused thumb. "I can tell that wasn't easy to admit to me," he began. "Please know that I am aware of how much you are walking out on faith with me. With us. I will not cause you hurt or harm, Bobbie. I swear."

She released a long and unsteady breath as she turned her head and pressed a kiss to his palm.

Lincoln accepted two crystal flutes of champagne from the bartender, taking a sip from his as he turned to make his way back across the grand ballroom of the luxury Manhattan hotel for Cole and Jillian's wedding reception. Every inch of the massive space had been converted to a beautiful floral wonderland.

"Good to see you, son," Phillip Senior said, stepping in Lincoln's path in a finely tailored gray tuxedo.

"Same to you, Phillip," he said.

"Have you thought more about accepting a position at Cress, INC.?" his father asked.

Lincoln looked across the ballroom at Bobbie in a circle with the bride, Raquel and four other women as they held hands dancing as Cole and his brothers looked on with smiles.

With Bobbie in his life for real, the idea of living in America was more appealing. But it was too soon to commit to that. There was so much to consider.

He took in Bobbie in a metallic beaded miniskirt and matching crop top with her wild hair bouncing about her as she danced. It reminded him of the 1970s' "Queen of Disco" Donna Summer's iconic look. And the smile on her face was pure and infectious. Joy burst from her like a glow.

"I'm seriously considering it," Lincoln admitted.

As the song ended, Cole danced over to his Jillian, who was radiantly beautiful in a sheer blush gown as her new husband pulled her into his embrace under the sparkle-filled spotlight. And when Cole held the face of his bride with both hands to kiss her, Lincoln saw the love he had for her on full display.

At that moment, his woman looked over at him and their eyes locked. His heart felt caught in a vise as she gave him that mischievous smile of hers. His entire body felt flooded with warmth.

Not the heat of desire, but something else. Something deeper.

"Lincoln," Phillip Senior continued. "I am not a perfect man—not even a perfect father—but I love my sons. I push them because I want the best for them—and I want to know that long after I'm gone, they will remember those hard taught lessons and cling to them."

Lincoln straightened his back and took the few steps to close the gap between them. He reached to clasp his father's broad shoulder with a tight grip as he peered into his eyes. "Is that what this race to the CEO seat is about?" he asked, his voice deep and demanding. "Are you okay?"

Phillip pressed his lips closed into a thin line.

"Please don't stand there after I lost my mother and lie to me about losing you too. I am asking you to trust me with the truth right now and not disrespect me with a lie," Lincoln demanded. "Are you okay?"

His father's expression became grim. "No," he admitted, shifting his gaze away.

"What's wrong?" Lincoln asked, surprised by the affection he felt for this man he still barely knew but was his sire nonetheless.

"Weak heart," he confessed.

The thought of losing him when he just found him shook him to his core.

"I'm not going anywhere just yet but my cardiologist wants me to slow down," Phillip Senior said.

Lincoln opened his mouth.

"I see you have questions, but not now. Not here. Not tonight, Lincoln," Phillip Senior said. "And let me be the one to tell your brothers."

His father gave him a stern look as he briefly squeezed his shoulder before walking away with long strides.

Lincoln downed the first flute of champagne and then the other as his thoughts raced.

What is the prognosis?
Why hasn't he stepped down yet?
What does this all mean?

Bobbie saw the grim look on Lincoln's face as he watched his father walk away from him. She was flooded with curiosity that quickly became concerned when he downed both flutes of champagne in rapid succession. She scooped up her gold clutch from the chair where she left it and moved through the sizable crowd to reach him.

"Something wrong, Lincoln?" she asked.

He took her hand in his and entwined their fingers before raising it to press a warm kiss to the back of hers. "Have a lot on my mind," he said.

"Anything you want to talk about?" she asked, pressing a kiss to his jawline.

"Not yet," he admitted.

"Is there anything you can do to fix it tonight?"

Lincoln shook his head.

Bobbie eased her arms around his waist and looked

up into his handsome face. "And is there anything I can do to help you?"

Lincoln looked down at her and smiled—a little. "If you could, you would. Right?"

Bobbie swayed her hips to the music. "In a heartbeat. Without question," she told him truthfully.

And she would.

Lincoln Cress had become a very important part of her life. A priority.

And every day he made her feel that she was of the same importance to him. She hated to think of his imminent return to England.

"Dance with me," she said.

Lincoln frowned. "I don't dance," he objected.

She took each of his hands into her own and walked backward to guide him onto the crowded dance floor. "I've seen your hips in action. Trust me—you can dance."

"I didn't say I can't dance. I said I don't dance," he corrected.

Bobbie raised one of his hands high in the air. "But I love to dance, Lincoln," she said. "And if I can ride a roller coaster with you, then *you* can dance with *me*."

Lincoln chuckled. "I knew that would come back and bite me in the ass," he mused.

"That moment is now," she said before clamping her teeth down to take a bite of air.

Lincoln shook his head as he began to two-step in sync to the music with her. Bobbie loved it and moved close to drape her arms around his neck as they swayed to the upbeat music together. He wrapped his arm around her waist and quickly tasted her mouth with a kiss. She rubbed the back of his head before she leaned in closer. "Thank you for helping me push against my fears—first on that roller coaster—and then taking that big leap to be with you. I don't regret either one because of you," she whispered near his ear. "Not one bit."

Conquering fears was not easy and the trepidation she felt about amusement parks' rides used to make her knees tremble. Until Lincoln. Sometimes she still wondered that she had ridden that roller coaster with him. That moment would always mean so much to her.

Lincoln gripped her tighter and picked her up on the dance floor. "I've got you," he promised.

She believed that.

Lincoln stood on the balcony with others enjoying the bottle of hundred-year-old scotch he gifted Coleman. The sounds of music and laughter filtered through the closed French doors and battled with the sounds of New York that were becoming all too familiar. "The city is really magnificent at night," he said, looking at the millions of lights scattered about the darkness.

"Sounds like our big brother has fallen in love with the Big Apple," Gabe said, twirling the aged alcohol in his snifter.

"Or *someone* in the Big Apple," Sean mused with a mischievous twinkle in his eyes.

Lincoln said nothing but looked back over his shoulder to exactly where he knew Bobbie was located. He stiffened and frowned to see her talking to Nicolette. Knowing the two women's feelings for each other were still very contentious, he took a large step to leave the balcony and head straight to them.

A strong hand gripped his upper arm to stop him.

It was Phillip Junior.

Lincoln's face filled with fury as he eyed his *little* brother.

"It's just Bobbie's turn," Phillip Junior explained after releasing him.

"Bobbie's turn?" Lincoln asked in confusion.

Gabe nodded as he gripped his snifter. "We've come to learn that our mother has a foolish proclivity for confronting every woman one of her sons becomes involved with," he said, still not seeming pleased with it.

Coleman snorted in agreement. "*Very* foolish," he muttered into his drink.

"It's like she feels challenged as the lone woman in the family and is afraid her position will be threatened," Phillip Junior said. "Trust me. She trapped Raquel in a corner early in our relationship and they are only close now because of our daughter."

Lincoln turned back to watched the women.

"Here's the thing—to be a part of this Goliath of a family the right woman will have to know how to handle our mother—"

"*The* Nicolette Lavoie-Cress," the other brother proclaimed in unison.

"In her own way," Phillip Junior finished.

"I'm just looking forward to the right one to tell her the right thing to make her stop the madness," Coleman said coming to stand beside Lincoln and look through the window panes of the French door at the women. "And maybe your little PI is just the one."

All six brothers now stood together and looked on as Bobbie reached to give Nicolette's elbow a light squeeze and offer a tight smile before she strolled away with a smug look.

Lincoln knew the look of satisfaction well and he

knew Nicolette may very well be regretting her decision to go toe-to-toe with *his* little private detective.

Nicolette turned to observe Bobbie's retreat and her face was one of pure frustration for a brief moment before she regained the composure for which she was well-known.

"Gentlemen, looks like we might have a winner," Coleman declared with his usual snark.

"I think she means well," Lucas offered.

Five pairs of eyes pierced him.

"Just because you're her favorite, *baby* brother, you don't have to defend her when she's clearly wrong," Sean said.

Lincoln's eyes sought Bobbie and he relaxed to see her enjoying herself without any loss of glimmer to her smile.

"I guess you have truly been accepted by *the* Nicolette Lavoie-Cress," Phillip Junior said.

The other brothers all chuckled, but Lincoln studied him. "And you?" he asked with seriousness. "Have *you* accepted me?"

It was Phillip Junior's turn to be judged as his brothers all cast him with pointed stares.

"I grew up with four brothers. Would *you* be happy to discover there's another one?" he asked, splaying his large hands.

"Growing up an only child, I was happy to find out I have five more," Lincoln countered, accepting he had not received a true answer from him.

He moved to pick up the bottle of scotch from where they'd set it on the floor of the balcony out of harm's way. He moved to each brother to top off their glass.

"First. Here's to Coleman's marriage to Jillian lasting longer than the age of the scotch," he said, raising his snifter high into the air with Manhattan as his backdrop.

The men all agreed and raised their glasses as well.

"Second. Here's to the Cress brothers," Lincoln said, thankful for the bond that had grown between them.

"To the Cress brothers," they all said in unison.

Bobbie enjoyed the feel of the water beating down against her skin as she inhaled the eucalyptus-fueled steam of the shower from the wreath hanging over the showerhead. She had contemplated taking a long soak in her bathtub, but the late hour had made the task seem too daunting.

Lincoln walked into the bathroom. "What *exactly* did you say to Nicolette?"

She smiled, remembering the moment all too well...

Bobbie had just stepped off the dance floor to take a break and reclaim her seat at their table. She had barely touched her heel to the carpeted area when Nicolette stepped in her path with a stiff smile.

"Are you ready for that talk now?" Bobbie asked, quickly snatching the upper hand.

Nicolette's brows raised. "It seems you are always ready for every...opportunity," she said.

"You know, sometimes people who see the worst in others are just reflecting the worst in themselves. You assume I would do something because you know *that you would," Bobbie said.*

Nicolette's eyes glistened with fury. "Nothing has a stronger pull for all sorts than money. Wealth. Clout," she said. "Must be difficult investigating the wealthy.

Playing dress-up in their lives and then going back to yours which is very different."

"Yes, my life is very different because unlike you I am not a woman who grew up in poverty and now acts like a rabid dog to protect the wealth you had to get used to," Bobbie assured her with a true smile, remaining unmoved from her peace. *"Nicolette, we are not the same. Let me introduce myself to you because it's clear you're clueless and making incorrect assumptions. I am Bobbie Barnett. Owner of B. Barnett Investigations with more than fifteen agencies under my belt and one hundred detectives across the country on my payroll—an empire left to me upon my father's retirement."*

Nicolette almost covered her shock well.

"I grew up in abundance and created even more, so the very last thing I am is in search of it through someone else. Nor does integrity allow me to betray Lincoln so I'm sorry but I'm not your leak," she continued, reaching quickly to give the woman's elbow a quick squeeze as she smiled at her. *"Now you have a blessed night and I hope you have learned once and for all to stop confronting people and assuming you will not get your feelings hurt. Or worse. Goodbye."*

And with that, she had walked away...

Bobbie wished she could find amusement in Nicolette's shock or care that although Nicolette was annoyed that she has also gained the woman's respect.

"Nothing, really," Bobbie lied as the glass door opened and a nude Lincoln stepped in behind her as steam escaped.

She turned and drew her hands down his hard chest and rigid abdomen. Her sighs of pleasure blended with the steam as he ran his fingers through the waves and then tilted her head back to wet it under the shower spray. He pressed kisses from her upturned chin to her mouth as she felt his erection snake up her belly with his arousal.

She loved that he never seemed to get enough of her. His hunger matched her own.

"I hate that you're leaving tomorrow," she admitted against his mouth.

"Two weeks," he reminded her of their plans for her to fly to London.

"Two weeks," she repeated as he lifted her by her waist.

Bobbie clutched to him as he sucked one of her tight brown nipples into his mouth. She pressed kisses to the top of his head as their heat mingled with the steam. The muscles of his back became her playground as he dug his fingers into the soft flesh of her buttocks to guide her core down onto his hardness. Inch by inch.

"Lincoln!" she cried out as she buried his face against his neck with a swear.

With her back pressed to the wall, as the water beat against his back and buttocks, Bobbie slid her arms up the wall as she rotated her hips to slide up and down the length of him.

The water poured down on Lincoln's head and chest as he watched her with a savage growl and bite down on his bottom lip. "So damn beautiful," he said, before using his strength to turn her body upside down against his.

He buried his face against her core and tongue kissed her throbbing bud with the cheeks of her buttocks sandwiching his cheeks. The tip of his hardness lightly tapped against her face and Bobbie turned her head to take it into her mouth.

Together, lost in their pleasure, they both sought and gave each other explosive climaxes as the water washed over their bodies, leaving them trembling and praying not to slip in the shower as they fell together into the white-hot abyss.

Nine

Two weeks later

There was a first time for everything.

As Lincoln took in Bobbie's profile, he knew that he was seeing her hurt and enraged as they sat on the sofa of his living room. As they planned she had arrived for her visit to St. Ives, but things had taken a turn for the worse.

"Bobbie," he said, reaching for her hand.

She slapped it away as she stared at him. In the brown depths were turbulence and unhappiness. He could so clearly see that she wanted to slap him or fall into his arms in tears.

And that tore at his gut.

Even as her mouth—that beautiful mouth that he loved—curled in what could be disgust, one tear raced down her cheek.

Damn.

Her face crumbled and the tears fell in earnest, but she didn't collapse against him for comfort and protection. Instead, she rose from the seat and crossed her arms over her chest to hug herself as her head hung as low as it could go.

Lincoln didn't know whether to go to her or leave her be. "Bobbie, please understand—"

She held up her hand and turned to look over at him with a bitter smile.

He hated that he did that to her—whether intentional or not.

Forgive me.

"How far along is she?" she asked, her voice hollow. Gone was her joy.

"Four months," he answered.

She closed her eyes before covering her face with her hands. It was clear that they trembled.

He did rise to go to her and take her body into his arms. She pushed against him. Against the normal. Hugs used to be constant. Affection plentiful.

Everything—*everything*—between them had changed.

Lincoln went back to the sofa to sink onto it before holding his head with his hands. It was mind-blowing how a phone call and five words from his ex Raven had effectively blown up his life.

I'm pregnant with your baby.

Even amid his concern for Bobbie, Lincoln felt flooded with emotions and the most prevalent one was guilt.

In the second after the words left Raven's mouth, he felt immense regret that this woman carried his child.

Not happiness at a new life. Or pleasure at having his first child. Or a sense of pride at continuing his legacy.

And for that, it took him back to a childhood flushed with feeling his father regretted him.

My hypocrisy.

"Damn," he swore, leaning back and covering his eyes with one of his forearms.

He knew he would love his child. Care for his child. Raise his child.

But that millisecond reaction was something he would carry with him forever.

"Congratulations," Bobbie said.

He raised his forearm and turned his head on the back of the chair to look at her. She leaned against the stone wall with her arms still crossed over her chest and her eyes brimming with emotion. "Bobbie—"

She shook her head in woe. "I knew it was too good to be true," she said softly, forcing a smile. "I knew *you* were too good to be true."

"Bobbie, I never cheated on you. This happened before we even knew each other," he explained for the dozenth time, needing her not to look at him with a new vision that pained him.

Disappointment.

"What do you want from me?" she asked, her face incredulous.

Lincoln pressed upon her with his eyes. "To not walk away from us," he said, knowing that losing her was more than he could bear.

The silence that followed was awkward.

"I want you in my life, Bobbie. Nothing can or will change that," he stressed, ensuring his eyes were filled with that truth.

Because of his desire to be with Bobbie and awareness of his father's illness, Lincoln had decided to hand the executive position of SHORES to his sous chef and move to New York. Just the night before they had celebrated his news with champagne-fueled sex.

"Your child will need you," she said. "So the move is off. Of course."

Of course.

That he knew. He had to be a daily influence in the life of his child and that could not be done from abroad.

"Absolutely and he or she will lack for nothing," he promised her and himself. "But I have just as much to offer you as my woman—my future, Bobbie."

Again, she shook her head. Denying him that hope. Something akin to panic gripped him. It was tight and unrelenting.

And unfamiliar.

"Bobbie, I will figure this out. I will make it work. I will do whatever it takes to have you in my life," he said, rising to cross the room to stand before her and grip her elbows as he bent his head to rest atop hers. The familiar sweet scent of her tore at his gut.

Just when he thought he would rise every morning with that scent by his side.

"How?" she asked. "I live there and you need to be here."

"And we will do what we were doing anyway. Make it work."

Bobbie's eyes studied his face. "But now *everything* has changed, Lincoln," she said.

"Only if we let it."

"That's easy for you to say," she countered with pained eyes. "Another woman is carrying your child."

True.

Bobbie shifted from his touch and walked over to the glass door where she pushed her bare feet into the slides she left there earlier. "I need some time alone, Lincoln, and so do you," she said.

And he did.

There was a lot to grapple with. Fatherhood. A renewed connection with a woman he never planned on having a future with. A child. Responsibilities. Sharing with his son or daughter what he never had from his father.

He watched Bobbie walk out of the house, across the deck and eventually reach the beach that was transformed by yet another beautiful sunset. They'd planned to walk the beach to reach his restaurant for dinner. Now he wasn't even sure if they would finish their vacation together.

Or have a relationship at all.

No, that can't be. Not when everything was breaking through for us.

It was all so cliché.

Lincoln eyed his wine cabinet and bar but had no thirst for alcohol. Nor food. Nor sleep. He crossed the length of the house and went out the rear entrance to the smaller deck and heated pool. Quickly, he removed the V-neck T-shirt he wore with linen shorts to plunge beneath the depths naked. It was just the shock he needed. As his arms slashed the water, he ate up the length of the narrow pool with them before turning and pushing off the wall with his feet to lunge forward and do it in the opposite direction. And then again. And again.

When he finally emerged, the skies were a myriad of vibrant colors and his thoughts had cleared. Decisions had been made. He climbed from the pool with ease, with water rolling and dripping off every inch of his frame. Without a towel handy he shivered because St. Ives nights still had a nip in the air, even later in May. He pulled on his shorts and padded barefoot into the house to check if Bobbie had yet to return.

We will figure this out.

In the bedroom, he grabbed a T-shirt and a hoodie to pull on over his head and changed into jogging pants before walking back across the house to go in search of her. He made it a quarter of a mile down the stretch of the private enclave of the beach and found her sitting atop a large piece of driftwood. The wind blew her hair and the edge of her peach twisted maxi skirt with a high slit that she wore with a matching tank crop top. When she rubbed her bared arms for warmth, he removed his hoodie and handed it to her when he reached her side.

"Thanks," she said, accepting it from him.

That made him hopeful.

"Let's head back to the house. It's chilly," he said, feeling a cool breeze attack him.

She pulled the hoodie over her head and was nearly overtaken by its size. They fell in step together. Neither shared their thoughts.

In the distance, Lincoln spotted a bird soaring across the tinted skies and dipping down to land in a tree. He assumed it was a raven because he had seen plenty in the area. He tried to avoid the bird's symbolism of loss and death.

"I'm going home, Lincoln," she said, as the lights from the beach house radiated like a beacon against the growing darkness.

He stopped walking and when she continued moving

forward away from him, Lincoln reached to clasp his hand around her wrist to stop her. "Bobbie, baby, don't do this," he said. "Who would have guessed that we would make it from where we started to where we are?"

"How sweet."

They both turned their heads at the sound of the voice.

He tensed at the sight of Raven standing on the deck. Bobbie pulled away from his touch.

"I thought we needed to talk and you didn't call me back," she said, her eyes shifting from him to Bobbie and back again.

Lincoln's eyes went down to her belly in the sundress she wore. It was still flat but soon would swell with his child. "I agree we need to talk," he said. "But this is not a good time, Raven."

Bobbie gave him a long look before she continued to the walking path and then up the steps to walk past Raven and enter the house.

Damn.

Lincoln rubbed his brows as he continued forward to the deck. "We have five months to go before the baby arrives, Raven. Pop-ups are not a part of the mix," he said. "But let me be clear, your pregnancy does not give you free license to my home or my life. I will be there for you. I will support you in this. If you or the baby is in harm, I will run to you and protect both of you. That is now my job, but I am also setting boundaries that you need to respect, Raven."

"You didn't call me back," she repeated.

"I was going to," he said truthfully. "I needed time to get used to the idea of becoming a father—"

"And to convince your girlfriend not to be jealous," Raven added as she pressed a hand to her belly.

Lincoln gave her a hard stare and felt even more regrets. "My woman. We're grown," he said. "And she has no reason to feel jealous. She is everything I want and need."

Raven took a step to close the gap between them. "*After* your child," she said.

Lincoln stepped back from her intrusion into his personal space. "Are you here to say something useful or to stir up drama?" he asked as he used his phone to summon a rideshare for her to get back home safely. "Matter of fact, Raven, you have a good night. Call me when you schedule your next doctor's appointment."

"You're going to it?" she asked, her face a mask of surprise.

"Of course," he said.

"I have this for you," she said reaching into the cross-body purse she wore to remove a piece of paper to hand to him.

Lincoln took it and looked at the 4D ultrasound, "Thank you," he said, feeling regret that his child would never meet his mother.

A baby. My baby.

"We'll have to celebrate," Raven said, coming over to wrap her arms around one of his as she looked down at the ultrasound.

Lincoln swiftly disengaged himself from her, worried about making a mistake. "I don't want to lead you on, Raven. The baby will not unite us into a relationship. We will co-parent respectfully but nothing more than that. Ever."

"In time—without pretty distractions," she said, with

a look inside the house. "You'll see that a *family* dynamic is best for *our* little Lincoln Junior."

He frowned. Deeply. "Like Lincoln Senior he will adjust to another dynamic," he drawled.

Lincoln was certain he didn't want to share his life with Raven. Of that, he was clear and unmoving.

Bzzzzzz.

He checked his phone. "Your ride is here," he said, carefully guiding her by the elbow off the deck and down the path around the house to the sloped driveway where a small green car awaited her. "Within the next few weeks I'll be in touch to discuss any financial assistance you'll need for doctor's appointments or medicine," he said after confirming the driver's identity.

"A-a-a-a few weeks," she sputtered as he opened the rear door and helped her inside the car, and firmly closed the door.

"Text me to let me know you got home safely," he said, lightly tapping the top of the car.

With his hands pressed deep into the pockets of his pants, he watched as the vehicle was reversed onto the cobblestone road before accelerating forward.

The ache was nearly unbearable.

Bobbie felt consumed by the steady throb of hurt, disappointment and an all too familiar fear that she foolishly thought she had conquered. Her past healing from that broken place felt fresh and radiated. Her anger at herself for exposing herself to this pain again was deep.

And the pain was deeper.

The scent of Lincoln's cologne clung to the hoodie and for a second, she pressed her face into the cloth and inhaled of it from where she sat on the low-slung sofa.

Everything was different.

She rushed to pull his clothing over her head to fling it away from her to the floor. Digging her fingers into the depths of her hair she massaged her scalp and released long unsteady breaths as she fought to reclaim her peace. Balance.

Instead, it felt like every step she took to heal, rise above and repair her broken pieces had disappeared, leaving her free-falling. And lost. So very lost.

Damn.

Just when she had begun to dream about forever with Lincoln.

And babies. Our babies.

Bobbie looked up just as Lincoln stepped inside the house. Her eyes dropped to the ultrasound picture he held in his hand. "I know how important this is for you, especially with everything you and your mom went through," she said, hating the hollowness in her voice.

Ashamed of her jealousy.

Fraught with her desire to unleash her anger. Break things. Scream. Act a fool.

Lincoln looked down at the image. "Thank you," he said.

"But we're over," she added, her voice firm even as her insides figuratively crumbled.

"No. I will fly to New York every damn weekend if that's what it *takes*," he emphasized.

"I can't. It *hurts*, Lincoln," she admitted in a whisper, lowering her head until her hair blanketed her face.

"You act as if I did something wrong intentionally," Lincoln said.

"You did! You didn't strap up with a woman you had no intention of building a life with," Bobbie retorted with her hand slashing the air as she pointed at him accusingly.

Lincoln pierced her with a cold stare.

Bobbie took the position on the sofa that he'd held earlier with her and lay back with her forearm over her eyes. "It would be great if yet another man in my life was not having a baby with someone else," she said before lowering her arm to look over at him just as his face hardened.

"You're not being fair, Bobbie," he said. "Our situation and the betrayal you faced with your husband are not the same. You're putting the weight of what he did on me. You are making me guilty or culpable for what your ex-husband did to you."

Bobbie jumped to her feet with her heart pounding as she pointed an accusatory finger at him "And you *knew* about it. You were fully aware of that before you even approached me about a relationship. Since you were aware of what broke me in my marriage, and then broke me down again as his mistress is now his pregnant wife, how can you not understand that for me *this* is too much to bear?"

The hard lines of his face softened with understanding before he hung his head.

"Do you know how it feels that someone else is carrying your child?" she asked, holding back none of the emotions raging inside her from her face. Her voice. Nor her eyes. "To love you and know someone else has that right. That duty. That gift."

He looked up. "You love me?"

With all my heart.

"Like a fool," Bobbie said, truly feeling like one for

setting aside every safeguard she put in place to avoid more heartbreak. "Once again loving the wrong man."

She saw a light in his eyes dull at her words, and that pained her but she could only speak her truth. At that moment they needed transparency more than ever.

"And what makes me the wrong man?"

"That you did not come to me free and clear of any obligations—including making sure when you left your previous relationship that there were no ties," she said, turning her head to land her eyes on the ultrasound. "Just like I shouldn't have gotten into a relationship before I was ready. That was the tie I brought into this. I am not over my divorce. I knew that. And I apologize for bringing that baggage with me into our relationship. I can accept my wrong in this. I wasn't ready and I knew that."

Bobbie twisted her mouth and shook her head as tears rose and quickly fell. And when Lincoln crossed the room to hold her, she did not fight him off. She welcomed what would be their last embrace. She allowed herself to snuggle her face against his neck and inhale deeply of his scent. It was a bitter irony that their bodies fit so well together.

And even in the midst of her hurt and disappointment, her body buzzed with awareness of his closeness. Everything tingled and awakened.

I will miss him so much.

"I'm not giving up on us," he swore as he pressed a kiss to her temple.

She lost count of how long they stood there with him holding her like he was afraid he would never get the chance again. With each passing moment, her heart continued to shatter because there was nothing more she wished than she'd met Lincoln Cress in another place. At another time. Before the heartbreak. Before he'd even met Raven. And then maybe, just maybe, they would have had a chance.

But that was not their reality.

"Don't leave early, Bobbie," Lincoln pleaded as he looked down at her and tilted her head back to run his fingers across her scalp amidst the wild waves of her hair. "Let's take a breath. Sleep on it and talk again in the morning."

Her eyes searched his as she forced a smile. "I'm going to turn in," she said, tired of the myriad of feelings flooding her.

She turned from him. His hand caught her wrist.

"Bobbie," he said, his voice deep and serious.

But she did not turn back. Tears she couldn't hold in raced down her cheek. Pain was once again her constant companion.

"Promise me we'll talk about this tomorrow?" he implored.

Bobbie nodded, but that wasn't to answer his question. She wanted to be let go. To be alone. To fight, once again, from having old wounds reopened and new wounds created.

She walked away quickly and felt relief as she stepped into the bedroom and closed the door to lean back against it. Her hands trembled as she locked the door.

Damn. Damn. Damn.

She moved over to the bed to fall atop it and clutch pillows to her chest as she curled her body into a ball and released her cries.

Of hurt.

Of bitter disappointment.

Of anger.

She had truly thought that things with Lincoln would work—much like she had assumed her marriage to Henny had been working.

In time—without pretty distractions. You'll see that a family dynamic is best for our little Lincoln Junior.

From inside the house, Bobbie had overheard Lincoln and Raven's conversation. And although he set boundaries, Raven made it just as clear that she was willing to break through them.

Yet another reason why Lincoln's pending fatherhood was more than she was willing to take on.

Long after her cries lost their ferocity and settled down to gentle tears, Bobbie lay there looking out the window. First, Henny hadn't wanted a baby with her and was having one with another woman. And now so was Lincoln.

The scent of him rose from the pillow and Bobbie snatched it from under her head and flung it away as if offended by it.

The knob rattled.

She flopped over onto her back to eye the door as her heart pounded, knowing Lincoln had just discovered that she did not want to share the bed with him.

He tried turning the knob again.

Bobbie sat up on the bed and pulled her knees to her chest to wrap her arms around her legs. She waited. For a knock. For him to call her name.

But nothing came.

Enough time passed where she knew he had walked away. She relaxed her body.

Hours went by. She moved about the room—to stand

at the window, to lie across the foot of the bed, to stare at her sad reflection in the bathroom mirror. She was tired but sleep was elusive. The waking hours were troubled but offered her clarity. Her mind was made up.

As the sun began to rise, Bobbie threw her clothing into her suitcase and called for a rideshare. She left the room with the case in hand. Lincoln's snores echoed from where he slept sprawled on the couch. She paused and looked down at him, even fighting the urge to wipe a bit of drool from his open mouth. And even that not dimming how handsome he was.

With one last look, Bobbie walked outside to the road to await her rideshare. She was thankful when it finally came and she was able to climb inside to be driven away, leaving Lincoln behind for the new life he had to build with the mother of his child and the baby who was on the way.

Ten

Three months later

Bobbie slowly walked every square inch of the penthouse terrace suite of the luxury Midtown Manhattan hotel with her arm outstretched with one of her handheld devices used to detect hidden cameras and bugging apparatuses. With over two thousand square feet and two levels, the work to ensure the privacy of her A-list client was slow and tedious. But necessary.

B. Barnett Investigations had numerous high-profile clients who required such service and it was well-known within the industry that their expertise was top-notch. After a full sweep and thorough background check of any hotel employees assigned to staff the five-figure-a-night suite, Bobbie was ready to give the "all clear."

She closed her eyes. For a moment, everything *almost* felt normal.

Almost doesn't count.

Bobbie shook her head to free it of the lyric from the singer's Brandy song of the same name.

She still missed Lincoln.

Thought of him.

Wanted him.

Loved him.

Even as she ignored his calls, blocked his texts, gave away the flowers he sent and pretended she was fine when she wasn't.

The time apart from him, and the depth of the ache of her heart, had proven that in such a short amount of time she had fallen in love with him. And it was an emotion more profound and mature than what she had with Henny.

More passion.

More respect.

More communication.

More fun.

The idea of that made her smile.

Lincoln being fun. Who knew?

But he had been. In *and* out of the bed.

And the sex. The most ridiculously *amazing* sex.

The passionate kisses.

The delectable sucks.

The addictive strokes.

So deep, long and hard.

Bobbie shivered and released a grunt of pleasure at the memory of it all.

She had restarted the clock on her year and found it far more difficult than after her breakup with her ex Henny. Though a good lover, he had never given her such explosive climaxes like Lincoln. The kind where you felt you teetered on the brink of blindness or a heart attack all while craving more of it. And Lincoln hadn't cheated on her and she felt him too honorable to ever do so. He never made her feel less than.

Quite the opposite…

One of Bobbie's favorite spots on the beach was the rope hammock that was suspended from the strong limb of a palm tree that hung parallel above the edge of the crystal-blue water. She had been in a strapless orange bikini reading a book on synchronicity while Lincoln grilled their lunch on the deck in the distance. She was looking forward to the meal of everything from the salad to the dessert cooked to perfection on the grill: roasted peppers stuffed with cheese and sausage, crispy sweet-and-sour pork belly skewers with bacon-wrapped Brussels sprouts, finished with macadamia-nut-crusted peaches and pineapple drizzled with brown sugar syrup.

Being with an acclaimed chef had its perks—and meant more exercise to beat off the decadent calories.

Feeling the sun's rays intensify, she worried about tan lines and removed her bikini top and bottom. "Better," she sighed in pleasure, arching her back and pushing her breasts higher into the air as she dropped a leg over each side of the hammock and let her feet dip into the warm water.

At the sound of a splash, she opened her eyes to see Lincoln swimming toward her with the speed of an Olympian as his muscled arms slashed through the water. She was surprised. He had just been on the dock but now here he was closing in. She smiled at the theme of Jaws *suddenly playing in her head.*

"Lincoln," she said when his head rose above the water.

"The sight of you naked drove me crazy," he said, rising to straddle the hammock.

Her eyes took in the sight of the water dripping off his muscles and down to his rising erection.

"We made love all night and then again this morning. There is no way you are riled up right now," she said.

"I will never *get enough of you," he swore before reaching to pull her body atop his lap and enter her swiftly with a deep thrust.*

The collective weights of their bodies had caused the secured hammock to dip into the water. The combination of their tempestuous thrusts and the splashes of the water rising to hit their bodies had been explosive.

And the food was great too.

But that was Lincoln. He constantly made her feel beautiful and desirable. With him, she always had his full attention.

Our situation and the betrayal you faced with your husband are not the same.

So true.

Finished with the first level elegantly decorated in pale gold and turquoise, Bobbie climbed the stairs to sweep the master bedroom and adjoining bath. She headed across over to the curtain-covered terrace. Once she was done, she could head home and—

And what?

Meditate? And visualize of Lincoln.

Sleep? And dream of Lincoln?

Take a bath? And touch herself while thinking of—

"Lincoln?" she said aloud as she eyed him standing in the center of the spacious terrace surrounded by both balloon and floral arrangements in pastel shades.

It was all so beautiful especially surrounded by the glass-and-metal skyscrapers with the sounds of NYC echoing in the air. But the most delectable sight was Lincoln. Tall, strong and handsome in linen slacks and shirt with polished leather shoes, belt and watch.

"Bobbie," he said, giving her a slow and warm smile that sent her heart off to the races.

"What's this about?" she asked coming to a stop before him.

They hadn't spoken in three months and his attempts to reach her had stopped a few weeks ago.

"This is about us sharing our life together. Loving each other. Creating memories—and beautiful babies," Lincoln began, as he lowered his body to his knees.

"No!" Bobbie shouted, more forcefully than she intended, as she grabbed his shoulders and failed at pulling him to stand back up.

"No?" he said in surprise as he rose to his full height on his own with his signature scowl back in place.

She'd missed it. "No," she said again softly.

"But the baby isn't mine—"

"What?" she said with eyes that quickly widened.

"Turns out there's another man back home in nearby Halsetown she also told was the father. He reached out to let me know she was double-dipping and we demanded a DNA test," he explained, reaching for her hand to take in his.

Raven's baby was not his.

She felt guilty at the pleasure that brought her.

Just horrible.

"Are you okay about it?" she asked, with true concern as she took the emphasis off herself and thought of him.

"I'm getting there. I've cycled through anger and disappointment more than a few times," he admitted.

"And for her to pull such a wicked stunt after losing your mom is just next level—"

"Horrific," he supplied, with a glint of some hard emotion in his eyes. "I had gotten used to the idea of having a child."

"Oh, *Lincoln*," she sighed, reaching to press her palm to his chest over his heart. "Your time will come."

He covered her hand with his own. "Yes. With *you*," he said, moving to bow again.

She shook her head and grabbed his shoulders again to stop him. "No, Lincoln," she stressed.

He scowled as he turned away from her to pace. "Why not?" he asked.

The irony of the sun setting and creating such a beautiful backdrop to the decorated terrace was not lost on her, especially as the solar lighting lining the space illuminated, giving the flower and balloon arrangements more depth and color. So utterly romantic.

And not apropos for the moment.

"Lincoln, I have missed you, and these last ninety days have been the most chaotic and heartbreaking in my whole life," she began, as she let her eyes follow him as he paced. "But nothing has changed for me."

He stopped and released a heavy breath as he studied her. "But you love me?" he asked, his voice tinged with sarcasm.

She nodded in earnest. "But for me, love is like the roller-coaster ride we shared—that mix of joy and mostly *fright* so I'm too afraid to enjoy the beauty of being high above trees," she said, wringing her hands and wishing the words she said were not true. But they were. "Love should be sweet and passionate. It should be a happy place. Somewhere where you get lost from the evils. The world's hardships have a little less bite because you know that you are wrapped up and protected by love."

"I am here. Moving to New York. Declaring I want to share my life with you and protect you. Prove to you that love can be everything that you're scared it won't be," Lincoln said, coming over to grasp her face with his hands as he ran his fingers across her scalp in a move that she had missed.

The shivers it brought were real.

"I am not Henny," he whispered down to her as they locked eyes.

"You are not Henny," she agreed softly. "But I'm still Bobbie and it's an everyday struggle with my fear that my heart will be broken. And I have not healed enough to take the chance again. My reaction to Raven being pregnant by you—"

"But she's *not* pregnant by me," he said, his eyes imploring her to understand. To accept.

Him.

His proposal.

His love.

And it was all so tempting.

It's no one's fault but my own. If I had just stuck to my one-year rule I wouldn't even know what I was missing about Lincoln...

She closed her eyes to break the hold as she struggled to explain what was heavy on her heart. "But my reaction to the news was so deep and visceral and maybe even more than it deserved but that was because of a broken place that I have not healed. That I *need* to heal, Lincoln. A foundation weakened by the past hurt of an old relationship was not the one upon which to build a new relationship."

"Bobbie," he said, bending to press kisses to her hairline.

For a moment, as her heart broke and temptation raged war with sensibility, she enjoyed the feel of his mouth on her skin and even turned her head to lock lips with his. And it was beautiful. The sweet beginning shifted to passionate heat and they clung to one another as their moans mingled in the heated air and rose to echo around them.

And just like their last embrace, she was so aware of how well their bodies fit together.

With every bit of strength, she could muster, she stepped back from him. "I can't marry you, Lincoln," she said in a voice barely a whisper as she continued to take backward steps away from him and all that he offered.

The thing was, that even at that moment all she could think of was that love was great when it was great but the flip side of that much love was profound pain and bitter disappointment when it all went wrong. The high wasn't worth the low. And she was just getting on the other side of her disappointment. And hurt.

With one last look back, she opened the French doors and left the terrace just as Lincoln removed the ring from his pocket and looked down at it with obvious regrets and a scowl that she had come to love.

She turned and grabbed the metal case holding her equipment before rushing across the bedroom and down the stairs to cross between the dining room and living room to the marbled hall and foyer. She opened the door but stopped in the doorway to find her father sitting in a Queen Elizabeth chair with a bucket of champagne and flutes on the table beside him.

"Dad," she said. "When did you get back?"

Bobby Barnett looked up from his phone. His broad and bright smile dimmed at her expression. Without words, she ran into the arms of the man whom she favored, and welcomed his embrace as her tears fell in earnest.

"You told him no," he said, his voice resigned.

She nodded against his barrel chest.

"You ready to talk about it?" he asked.

"Not yet," she said.

"You head home and I'm coming right behind you," Bobby said with a kiss to her cheek and comforting pats to her back.

She stepped from his hold and made her way down the hall to the elevator.

"Bobbie," he called behind her.

She stopped and turned.

"You love him?" he asked.

"Sometimes love isn't enough," she said.

Bobby shook his bald head. "Not your whole spiel on fear and heartbreak. Just plain and simple. Do you *love* him?" he asked.

He was always straight with no chaser.

Never had she lied to her father. Their bond was far too deep for that.

"Yes," she admitted. "But—"

"But nothing, Bobbie," he said.

"Daddy, I have not spoken to him in three months.

The last I heard he had a baby on the way. He hasn't even really said *I love you* to me," she spouted, finding weak excuses to not be judged for her choice at that moment.

"I hear all of that—sometimes we men get it wrong. We miss the cues. All of that. I get it. But he reached out to me. Asked my permission to propose like a gentleman. I gave it and helped set all this up. Let me just check on him too. Like a gentleman. Okay?"

That was her father. A tall and mighty man with a heart of gold.

Bobby opened the door to the suite. "I'll be to your place soon," he said, before stepping inside and closing the door.

Lincoln fought the urge to toss the costly ring over the side of the building as he was trying to reconcile just what went wrong. When wasn't love enough? With a frustrated sigh, he gripped the three-carat diamond ring in his fist.

Foolishly he'd thought it all would end in the big "happily-ever-after" moment. The kind in all the sappy romance movies. But that was how Bobbie made him feel. Soft, smiling and happy.

Currently, he was fighting a rising annoyance. Raven's pregnancy being an issue for her, he understood. Unfaithfulness had a way of skewing anything and everything for the person who suffered the betrayal. But it felt like she had more mistrust in Henny than trust in him.

Enough is enough.

Lincoln turned at the sound of the French doors

opening. "Bobbie," he said, but his disappointment came quickly at the sight of her father.

"Wrong one," Bobby said with a smile.

"There was a lot wrong about tonight," Lincoln said with snark.

Bobby walked over to the end of the terrace to look over the edge. "I think a lot went right, Brit," he said, reaching in his pocket to pull out a small pack of Peanut M&M's.

Lincoln sat on one of the padded chairs. "How?" he scoffed. "I'm on the terrace with the ring and her dad with her nowhere in sight."

Bobby chuckled. "Listen, I didn't leave my yearlong fishing trip—"

Lincoln scowled. "What's with you Barnetts and this year thing?" he asked.

"Two different things. Plus, *mine* is for enjoyment, Brit," Bobby said before tossing a red M&M into his mouth.

Enjoyment, Lincoln thought as he looked through the glass of the French doors at the king-size bed wishing Bobbie would soon be joining him.

But he couldn't tell her father the plans he had to sex his daughter. He hadn't been with anyone since Bobbie and didn't want anyone else since having her. He was not just hoping to start their forever but to take off the edge of his desire. Feeling randy was an understatement.

Looking for a diversion from his heated thoughts of her, Lincoln glanced up at the moon high above the energetic city. "Wait," he said, sitting up straight to look over at the man he hoped to be his father-in-law. "Brit, huh?"

"Ms. Pott fills me in on plenty," Bobby assured him

with a wink before walking over to claim the seat across from Lincoln. "And that's why *we* approve of you for Bobbie."

"Ms. Pott approves?" he asked, not hiding his surprise.

"You won her over."

"Thanks, but what matters is if Bobbie approves and tonight, she proved that she doesn't," he said.

"If you give my feisty daughter some time—don't chase her, don't call, let her miss you—then she will realize that a broken heart can mend and love again. *Then* you'll both have your happily-ever-after," Bobby advised.

Lincoln opened his hand and eyed the ring on the center of his palm. "Time?" he asked. "And if that doesn't work?"

Enough is getting to be enough.

Bobby rose to his full height. "Then it isn't meant to be," he simply offered. "Doesn't make either of you wrong, but it may mean you're not right for each other. It happens."

Lincoln continued to eye the ring he chose just for Bobbie. It was simple in design but fabulous with the many diamonds adorning the band.

Just like Bobbie.

She was a natural beauty. Not much makeup. Her hair was wash and go. Her clothes more about comfort than anything. And somehow her simplicity came off fabulous. Without her even trying.

Ironically, she was *trying* like hell to heal heartbreak and was failing miserably.

"I'd pay good money to get my hands on Henny Santana," he said, feeling the tightness of his jaw as he clinched and unclenched his fist.

Bobby grunted in scorn. "The fact that he's a cop is the only thing keeping me off his behind. *Trust* me," he said.

"She didn't deserve what he did to her—during the marriage or after," Lincoln offered. "So, I get it that my ex's pregnancy hit too close to home for her, but I honestly thought finding out it wasn't my baby would help."

"Give her time," Bobby said before another M&M joined the ones on which he was already chewing.

Lincoln outstretched his legs and crossed them at the ankles as he took in the sight of the towering skyscrapers glittering against the night sky. The sounds of traffic congestions, car horns and raised voices floated up into the air to echo around him. It was all so different from the solitude of the beach, but he needed to get adjusted because New York was now his home.

The revelation of Phillip Senior's illness—and his desire to spend more time with Bobbie—had motivated his decision to move to Manhattan the first time. Raven's pregnancy had halted his plan. The aftermath of discovering he did not have a child on the way had rocked him to his core. He had begun to look forward to holding his child, purchased gifts and made plans to reconfigure his home to have a nursery.

He attended prenatal appointments.

He supported her financially.

For it all to be exposed as a lie.

That hurt. He could admit that. And then he became furious for weeks after that.

When he emerged from it, he knew it was time to reclaim his life. His woman. His relationship with his father and his brothers. His happiness.

Forgiving the manipulations of a woman desperate

to have him had not been easy but he had gathered up all the toys and clothing he'd bought and dropped them off to her with clear instruction to never contact him again. His next stop was the airport for a ride on the Cress family private jet to reach America.

His sous chef had assumed head chef duties and running of SHORES. His beach house was secured and awaiting his arrival back to St. Ives for vacations. He was leasing a condo in Manhattan that would be ready in a couple of days. His family was pleased with his move—even Phillip Junior was warming up more.

The only thing missing is Bobbie.

That was a week ago and if he was honest, he did feel relief—not because he wouldn't be a father—but that Raven would not be the mother of his child. That was an honor he wanted for Bobbie.

"I love your daughter," Lincoln admitted.

"Tell *her* that."

Lincoln scowled. "You said to let her be. So when?"

"In time," Bobby said.

Lincoln sat up straight and eyed the other man. "Is time your answer for everything?"

"It heals all wounds," Bobby promised.

Bzzzzzz. Bzzzzzz. Bzzzzzz.

Lincoln removed his phone and smiled at an incoming FaceTime from Sean's number. "Excuse me," he said to Bobby before answering the video call. Nearly all the five faces of his brothers filled the screen.

"Congratulations!"

"Where's Bobbie?"

"How'd it go?"

"Show us the ring."

"I told them we'd be interrupting."

Lincoln could barely keep up with which brother said what.

Bobby stood up and walked around Lincoln's chair to regard the men on the screen. "Good Lawd, your daddy got strong genes!" he exclaimed.

All of them chuckled—and even those sounded just as similar as they were in looks.

"And it didn't go well, fellas," Bobby added.

Lincoln glowered at him.

Bobby shrugged and tossed another candy into his mouth.

"Bobbie just needs a little more time," Lincoln explained at their solemn expressions.

I hope.

"We're all at CRESS X having drinks. Come join us," Sean offered, focusing the phone on his face with the stylish bar of the restaurant in the background.

Bobby nodded his approval. "Go!" he mouthed as he pulled his cell phone from his pocket and began texting away. "Besides, I'll keep this suite for the night. Call a pretty lady friend and get your money's worth. I can *promise* you that."

Lincoln made a comical face of distaste, but he also found the man hilarious and had come to like him since his call to ask for permission to propose to Bobbie and then his help planning the engagement scene.

If the suite is thanks enough then so be it.

"In Tribeca? Right?" Lincoln asked Sean.

"Yup. We're waiting."

The screen went black when Sean ended the call.

"Suite's yours," Lincoln said, rising to his feet and sliding the ring back inside his pants pocket.

Ding.

Bobby glanced at the phone in his hand. "And so is Ms. Pott. For tonight," he said with a wolfish smile and wiggle of his bushy brows.

"Wait. What?" Lincoln said in shock. "You know what? Never mind."

Lincoln handed Bobby the suite's metallic key card. "The design decorator should be here in the morning to take all this down," he said walking over to open one of the French doors. He paused. "Thank you, Barnett. For the help. The advice. Hell, for raising one hell of a daughter."

"Save it for when I walk her down the aisle to you," Bobby said.

Right. It will happen. In time.

Lincoln wasn't giving up on Bobbie. Not yet. His heart wouldn't let him.

Eleven

One month later

Lincoln eased his hand into the pocket of the pants of his tailored suit as he stood on the glass terrace of the parlor floor of Gabe and Monica's new brick townhome in the West Village. He sipped from a flute of champagne and looked down upon the long and narrow landscaped backyard that had served as the setting of the couple's intimate wedding. It was far smaller than the reception of Cole and Jillian but just as beautiful with only family and close friends in attendance—less than twenty. Having gotten to know Gabe and Monica it was the ideal setting for them with more importance given to privacy than a grand event.

His grip on the glass tightened as his gaze fell on Bobbie—again.

It was hard to ignore her when she looked so radiant, especially lit by the glow of the candles on the six-foot-tall candelabras scattered amongst the white floral arrangements. And in her fuchsia halter dress that was tied at the waist—emphasizing her shape—she stood out among the crowd.

Or you can't take your eyes off her.

Before their appearance at the wedding that day there had been no change between them. It was the epitome of a standstill. No communication. No sight of her. No reconnections. Nothing.

Just serious thoughts on whether it was time for him to move on with his life.

Maybe even beyond time.

They had spent more months apart than they had as a couple.

Even during the festivities, they might occasionally share a look or awkward smile but neither had spoken a word to the other.

It seems time is not on my side.

"Lincoln."

He turned as Phillip Junior stepped out onto the balcony. He inclined his head in greeting. "Thanks for meeting with me. I need your help with something," he said.

Phillip Junior looked hesitant. "Okay," he said.

"Listen, I'm new to being a big brother and new to the family so I need your advice on how to handle a situation," he said.

"With the family or the business?" Phillip Junior asked.

Lincoln unbuttoned his jacket and leaned against the building. "Both."

His brother looked pensive.

"I have some news on our father that he asked me not to share so that he could tell you and the other brothers himself," Lincoln admitted. "But that was months ago and I feel guilty keeping it from the brothers."

"Why did he tell you and not us?" Phillip Junior accused with a narrow-eyed glare.

Lincoln sighed heavily. "He didn't tell me. He said something odd and I questioned him about it," he said, taking a deep sip of the amber liquid. "Please focus on the problem at hand. I thought we were moving beyond your issues with something neither of us can control— we share the same father."

Phillip Junior regarded him. "Put yourself in my shoes," he said, relaxing the lines of annoyance on his face.

Lincoln inclined his head. "I am. That's why I'm asking you for your help with this. Who better to know how to navigate our father than the son who has been with him the longest?" he asked, choosing his words carefully.

It was a symbolic olive branch, the symbol of peace and goodwill.

He had been officially appointed to his new position at the company and although he was enjoying the challenge of shifting the company's sustainability forward, things could go more smoothly. And that involved Phillip Junior. Short of knocking him off his feet with one solid punch, Lincoln knew if he was going to work at Cress, INC. and get anything accomplished he needed Phillip Junior as a friend and not foe.

"What's the secret?" Phillip Junior asked.

Lincoln knew he was betraying their father's confidence but had finally decided that truth was always the best course of action. "Phillip Senior is ill and that's why he will eventually step down as CEO of Cress, INC.," he admitted.

The expression on his brother's face shifted from confusion to concern.

Lincoln understood the apprehension all too well. "With discovering my mother didn't reveal her illness to me and how that made me feel in the days after her passing, I just can't sit with this info any longer and contribute to any of my brothers feeling the way I did *if* something was to happen unexpectedly," he explained.

Phillip Junior swore as he took a long step across the terrace to look down at his parents standing together as they studied a tray of heavy appetizers before making their selections. "Does my mother know?" he asked. "Wait. Of course, she does. They are thick as thieves about everything."

"Do you think he will eventually tell the family?" Lincoln asked. "And if not, what's the best way to tell the other brothers?"

Phillip Junior began to pace his tall and muscular frame. "No, he won't reveal it. He'll see it as weakness and that's not acceptable," he snapped in annoyance. "We'll have to tell the brothers and then all of us confront them if we ever want the truth."

"I agree," Lincoln said, watching as the other man finished his champagne and then grabbing his own glass to do the same.

"How serious is it?" Phillip Junior asked, his voice somber.

"I don't know, but it's enough for him to consider stepping down," Lincoln said, dropping his now empty hand.

Phillip Junior shook his head and frowned. "He loves this damn company so much he'll kill himself for it," he said, his words tinged with bitterness.

Lincoln scowled, recognizing that his brother's glare looked very much like his own. "No offense, Phil, but I assumed you would too," he drawled.

Phillip Junior looked surprised. "Me?" he asked.

"You're pretty cutthroat about wanting the position," Lincoln said gingerly.

"I am?" Phillip Junior said, considering that before finally chuckling. "I suppose I am. And don't you forget it."

"Let me make it clear that I am not interested in stepping in as CEO," Lincoln assured him. "I haven't been in the thick of it enough and will never catch up to the time put in by the rest of you so I'm not interested."

Phillip Junior smiled. It was large and toothy. "And then there were three."

Both Gabe and Cole had already made it clear they held no interest in the position for their individual reasons, leaving just Phillip Junior, Sean and Lucas in the running.

"Besides, I'm ready for more than a career," he said, as he turned to look for Bobbie just as she tossed that wild hair he loved back and laughed with a joy he wanted to share. "A family. A wife. Babies."

Phillip Junior came to stand beside him and follow his line of vision. "I was wrong about Bobbie," he admitted.

Lincoln grunted in agreement. "Yes, the hell you were," he said as he continued to enjoy seeing Bobbie again.

"Okay. I deserve that," Phillip Junior said with a

chuckle. "But let me say this. There is *nothing* better than coming home to Raquel and our daughter. It's a sweet spot. Sweetest in the world."

Bobbie looked up and froze to catch Lincoln's eyes on her.

His heart pounded when she didn't look away.

"That sweet spot you're talking about requires love and a desire to be that sweet spot," Lincoln said.

"Well big brother, if you can't tell that the look on that woman's face is love then you are the biggest fool of all," Phillip Junior said, clapping his shoulder with his hand.

Then why won't she fight for me?

With her face upturned and the candlelight flickering in her eyes, he didn't know if he'd ever seen her more beautiful. His heart swelled. His desire awakened.

"I love you," he mouthed, letting his conviction show on his face and his heart on his sleeve.

He saw that she gasped. That beautiful mouth quivered and her eyes filled with tears that he knew would haunt him. Without hesitation, Lincoln turned and headed inside the house to quickly walk around the landing that opened to the ground level below. He hurriedly descended the ornate stairs to the entry foyer. He passed the closed doors of both the powder rooms and closet on his left and then the elevator on his right before making short work of the kitchen, living room and dining room to exit the house into the rear garden.

He thought of his mother and missed her exuberance because she would have rooted him on.

In the open doorway, with his heart pounding from exertion and excitement, Lincoln looked for Bobbie. His eyes landed on every face. His brothers. Jillian.

Raquel and Collette. His parents. The judge who performed the ceremony. Monica's aunt Phoebe and her friends, Choice, Kylie, Nylah and Montgomery. Gabe's best friend, Lorenzo León Cortez.

But no Bobbie.

"She left as soon as you made a run for her," Phillip Junior said, easing past him to walk the length of the garden.

Still running away from me. To hell with this.

Lincoln couldn't deny his annoyance. His patience was wearing thin. He was a good man, but not perfect. If she was done then it was time for him to get on board with that.

Enough is enough.

He was done chasing or waiting or hoping.

Ding-ding-ding.

Still upset, with his all too familiar scowl back in place, Lincoln gazed at Gabe and Monica as she looked up at her husband as he dinged a fork against a crystal flute.

"Again, we thank you for being here to share this occasion with us," Gabe said with a smile. "We thought we would also share some more good news."

"We purchased the house and sold the condo because we are extending our family," Monica said while pressing her hand to her belly. "We're having a baby!"

Lincoln's coldness instantly thawed and he was able to muster a smile as Auntie Phoebe and Nicolette released shrieks of surprise and happiness. He moved forward to wait his turn to shake his brother's hand and bend to press a kiss to Monica's cheek. "Congratulations," he said with warmth.

"You okay?" Monica asked, locking her eyes with his as she pressed her palm to his cheek.

Like a sister.

They were all aware of his mother's death, Raven's duplicity and his breakup with Bobbie. He just didn't know if her concern was about Raven or Bobbie or his mom. Maybe a bit of all three. Either way, he was thankful that in her moment of celebration she thought about him.

"I'm good. I promise you," he swore. "But I am going to head home."

"You sure?" she asked. "Sometimes it's good to be around family."

"I agree," Gabe said.

"Just got a lot on my mind," Lincoln admitted. "But congrats again on the wedding, the house and the baby."

He gave them another smile that was forced before giving everyone a wave and turning away to leave. At that moment he knew he had to let go of Bobbie. Once and for all. Perhaps even time to begin dating another woman.

All of that would come, but for tonight he just wanted some quiet to let go of hope and let his heart break. Tomorrow he would begin to heal and perhaps one day love again. Unlike Bobbie, he was open to that.

Bobbie climbed from her vehicle and pulled on a lightweight trench because of the end-of-summer night breeze. In the distance, she looked at the towering one-hundred-and-twenty-five-foot roller coaster. The colorful lights lining all the rides lit up the night and the sounds of screaming, laughter and fun making clung to the air. She knew she looked out of place in her evening gown and heels, but when she ran from Lincoln like a child and drove the streets, she had the urge to go back to the place where she once was able to conquer a fear.

With Lincoln.

For Lincoln.

She crossed the parking lot and climbed the weathered wooden steps to the boardwalk. She stopped at one of the concessions stands for a strawberry-shortcake-flavored cotton candy. With one deep bite into the confection, she wiggled her shoulders in delight. It tasted almost as good as Lincoln looked at the wedding.

Like a fool, she had let her curiosity get the best of her.

After she turned down his proposal, Lincoln's attempts to reconnect came to an abrupt end. No more calls, text messages, flowers or other romantic gestures. No pop-up visits. Nothing. Not that she blamed him.

We're done.

Why should he fight for her when she long gave up the fight for him?

Why should he stay single when he was the walking epitome of great sex?

Why shouldn't he fall in love with someone not afraid to love him back?

As the days to the wedding had drawn near, Bobbie had wavered on whether to attend or not knowing Lincoln would there—maybe even with a date. But there had been no one with him. He looked *amazing*. And smelled just as good.

As she followed behind him and the other wedding guests down the hall to the dining room, she had passed through his lingering scent and inhaled it with a grunt of pleasure that drew the curious eyes of those beside her.

And although he kept his distance, his eyes were on

her. She felt the intensity of the stare and it caused fine hairs to rise on the back of her neck. And everything pulsed. Quicker. Harder.

Desire.

Frustrating, persistent, pulsing desire.

I'm a fool.

Ms. Pott thought so.

Her father told her so.

And her heart *knew* it to be so.

I love you, he had mouthed with every bit of the emotion in his eyes.

At that moment as tears welled, never had she felt more loved. Never. And when he turned to leave the balcony, she knew he was headed straight to her. To hold. To have. And she knew she would not be able to resist him. It.

That pulsing passion was ever-present.

And she ran.

But there was no escaping the love she felt or the desire he created.

Bobbie pursed her lips and released a long breath that did nothing to ease the hunger—nor did the lick she gave her cotton candy wishing it was Lincoln's lips instead. And chin. Chest. Belly. And down to every long and hard inch of his—

"That must be *really* good."

Bobbie froze with her tongue still extended and turned to find Lincoln standing behind her. Surprise was an understatement. And her heart thundered as she took him in, standing there with a black lightweight overcoat he wore over his tuxedo blowing in the wind. It reminded her of their meeting in front of The Met. He had been so handsome and sexy that night as well.

She thought of the time they shared, from being antagonistic to allies to friends, and then lovers. And now, in love. But apart.

Because of me.

"What are you doing here?" she asked, aware of the marvel in her voice.

Lincoln briefly looked down at his polished shoes as he took a step closer to her. "Honestly? I don't know. I was headed home and instead, I had the urge to come here," he said with a half smile and shake of his head as if he was as amazed by the coincidence.

Or was it a sign?

"Me too," she said.

"I was thinking about you and how you *keep* running from me and all this love I have for you, Bobbie Barnett," Lincoln admitted, tilting his head back to look up at the roller coaster. "And then I remembered just how brave you were that day you rode this monster with me."

Bobbie studied his profile and felt the hurt she caused him—and understood that in her haste to protect herself she had left him wounded. "Oh, Lincoln," she whispered.

He looked down to stare at her. "I just can't understand why you won't take my hand—like you did that day—and jump headfirst into this with me? What the hell, Bobbie?" he asked, his frustration causing his voice to swell.

They drew curious stares and he pressed his lips closed before wiping his mouth with his hand.

Bobbie raised her arms to weave her fingers through her hair to furiously shake it as a swirl of emotions wrestled her. Confusion. Frustration. Heart attack. Sadness. And yes, in the midst of all that was joy.

That was what loving Lincoln Cress was for her. Pure, unadulterated joy.

She added the drama. The negativity. The inability to hope for more. Because of her fears.

"I thought I needed to heal first. My reaction to Raven's pregnancy was a lot. But it wasn't about just you and Raven—that damn Henny is in the mix. And yes, I just realized that sounds like a cocktail, but *listen*—"

"You listen. Are you truly that bothered by your ex at this point or have you convinced yourself that's how you *should* feel?" Lincoln asked.

Bobbie opened and closed her mouth several times as she considered that.

Lincoln looked pleased with himself at her continuing silence.

She couldn't believe that they came to a place that held significance for them both at the same time. There was no way she couldn't believe it wasn't fate bringing them together. Like they were meant to be—a perfect alignment brought on by the universe for her greater good.

What better way to heal a broken heart than letting a good man pour real love—destined love—into it.

And it's been four months. I've barely thought of Henny or his new family. Be gone and be blessed.

The roller coaster came to a stop and they both looked up as the riders all screamed in fright or fun. She closed her eyes remembering how she felt being up there.

Open your eyes and enjoy the view, Bobbie. Trust me, please.

That memory of his British voice low and warm near her ear made her smile.

I just can't understand why you won't take my hand— like you did that day—and jump headfirst into this with me?

Bobbie took a deep breath and closed the gap between them with a step, to ease her hands around his waist. Lincoln leaned back a bit as if nervous about her next move. She chuckled. "I have a deal for you, Lincoln Cress," she began. "My heart, my soul and a yes to marrying me for one of your smiles."

Lincoln frowned. "No," he said, stepping back out of her embrace.

And that felt like an emotional death blow. "What?" Bobbie gasped.

Lincoln undid his bow tie and opened the top button of his shirt to remove a gold chain. At the end of it dangled the engagement ring. "I have worn this every day since that night you turned me down, hoping you would take the leap," he said as he removed it from the chain and lowered his body to one knee. "So, thanks for the offer, my love, but you do not get to steal this moment from me."

And it was Bobbie who smiled as he took her left hand in his and slid the ring to the tip of her finger. It just all felt so right. So natural—more so than them being apart. She had a lot of time to make up for.

"Bobbie Barnett, will you spend the rest of our lives loving me and sharing your life with me as I promise to never disrespect you, replace you or break you with *all* my heart and soul?" he asked.

She nodded eagerly, unable to speak words as her emotions overwhelmed her. Lincoln slid the ring on to her finger and then rose to pull her body up against his. She trembled with anticipation for the taste of his mouth and was not disappointed. "I missed you so much. For-give me," she whispered in between kisses as she held his handsome face with both of her hands.

"Love me. Have me," he countered before tracing her mouth with his tongue then deepening the kiss.

At the sudden burst of applause, Lincoln and Bob-bie looked around at the onlookers cheering on the pro-posal.

"Awwww. Thank you!" Bobbie said to them as Lin-coln swooped her up into his arms.

With long strides, Lincoln ate up the distance down the boardwalk to the parking area as Bobbie held on tightly to him and pressed kisses to his neck. In his em-brace, she felt like she was flying.

And when he lowered her to her feet with her back pressed against the doors of a Bentley SUV, she tilted her face up to look at him. Love on him.

"Listen, Bobbie, we will communicate and compro-mise together. Hell, we'll even go to therapy together if need be, but we do whatever it takes to be happy *to-gether*," he stressed before pressing heated kisses to her mouth.

"I agree," she said, rising on the toes of her shoes to deepen the kiss. "And I can think of something else we should be doing *together*."

His eyes lit with a whole new fire that made her shiver in anticipation. "Your place or mine?" Lincoln asked, his voice deep and very serious.

Bobbie wiggled her brows. "How about your SUV or mine?"

Lincoln looked dubious.

"It's been four months," she reminded him. "Four *long* and lonely months."

"True," he said, shifting his hips forward to press the length of his erection against her belly. "But—"

Bobbie's eyes widened in surprise—at the hard feel of him and his reluctance. "You've never?" she asked in disbelief.

"In a car?" Lincoln spouted. "No."

"Oh then we are doing this in *your* Bentley," she said, easing past him to open the rear door.

Lincoln looked around them as she climbed onto the rear seat, closed the door and lowered the window midway. "What are you doing?" he asked.

"Getting naked."

He frowned, but he also leaned in to take a peek.

Bobbie had stripped of everything but her lace panties. She eyed him with a stare that was a dare as she removed them slowly. "Get in," she said.

Desire was clear in the dark depths of her eyes but battled with his hesitation. Her reserved and proper British gentleman did not want to be naughty with her. She stretched the full length of her body with her eyes closed and her back arched into a curve.

Lincoln swore at the moment before she felt a gush of wind against her body. She smiled as he slid onto the rear seat and slammed the door closed as he pulled her body onto his lap to straddle. "Bobbie," he moaned against her cleavage before deeply sucking the soft swell of each breast as he rushed to remove his clothing.

The heat of his body against hers was intoxicating. The feel of his tongue on her taut nipples dizzying. And when he wrapped his strong arm around her waist, she felt him tremble in that hot moment just before he raised and then lowered her down onto his hardness. His heat. His thickness. The inches.

Damn.

Their gasps blended in the air as they clung to one another and fought for their climaxes not to explode too soon.

United once again.

She loved the way his eyes feasted on her body. The energy they created whenever they were near each other was ever-present, bouncing against the interior, charged with fiery sex and intensified by love, commitment and trust.

Bobbie leaned back a bit to look down at him as the stars and the moonlight illuminated them via the expansive moonroof. "I am thankful my fears were defeated by fate," she whispered against his mouth as she used her walls to clutch and release his inches. "You *are* the love of my life."

Lincoln let his head fall back against the rest and gave her a slow smile before he began to rotate his hips to glide up and down inside her. "I will love you always," he promised. "Always. Always. Always."

Bobbie released a sharp gasp as she matched his rhythm with the back-and-forth rock of her hips with her arms above her head and her hands pressed to the glass of the moonroof. She felt as if she floated amongst the stars and her cries of pleasure echoed against the moon. It was ethereal. She felt at one with the universe.

Epilogue

Four months later

The entire Cress family was solemn as they sat in the waiting room of the private hospital in Manhattan. Lincoln enjoyed the feel of Bobbie's body at his side with her head resting on his shoulder as she rubbed circles onto the back of the hand she held. Just like she had done for his mother's death, Bobbie was at his side providing comfort and care as they all awaited word of Phillip Senior's condition during a very risky cardiac surgery. Although it was him who needed comfort, he bent his head to press a kiss on her forehead.

"I love you, Bobbie Barnett-Cress," he whispered for her ears alone, thinking of their elopement in Las Vegas before traveling to their beach house back in St. Ives for a steamy honeymoon where nudity reigned.

She raised her head to look up at him, with her wild hair framing her face, and her eyes emotional with her feelings. "I know," she said, squeezing his hand. "I *know*."

And he did. Fully. Completely. Deeply.

And he knew that she felt the same. She let him know in a million different little ways.

They were great together and it was only just the beginning.

Now if things with our father could be going just as well.

He and Phillip Junior had joined forces as planned to meet up with the other Cress brothers concerning their father's failing heart. With unity, it was decided they would go to Nicolette first for the truth. And they did. And without much resistance, their strong and formidable mother had dissolved into tears. Her relief and need for help had moved them all because the weight of carrying the secret, the fear and the burden had become too much to bear.

Unfortunately, they were not as successful with the head of the family.

Instead of welcome and transparency, Nicolette and the brothers came against anger and belligerence—like the leader of a pack of animals losing his might and dominion. He had been enraged and his words biting as he lashed out at them for encouraging him to get the surgery recommended by a world-renowned cardiologist.

That had been four months ago.

Phillip refused to step down from the demands of being CEO. Refused to slow down. Change his eating habits. Control his temper. Rest. Have the surgery.

That morning the choice had been snatched away

from him when he was discovered passed out in the den of the family townhome. He'd been rushed to the hospital and then almost immediately after that into open-heart surgery.

That had been eight hours ago.

Nicolette stood by one of the tall and narrow windows, assumingly looking at the brutal winter storm that raged outside. Concern lined her face and aged her a bit beyond her sixty years. Although the heat was on, she gripped the edges of the silver fox she still wore as if holding on for dear life.

For more than forty years she loved Phillip Cress Senior and built a business and family together. They'd forgiven each other for things spoken—and probably unspoken. Known—and probably unknown. They stuck together through it all. With love.

The door to the waiting room opened. A woman in her mid-to-late forties, dressed in scrubs, entered. Everyone rose to their feet, including Monica who was seven months pregnant with twins.

"Comment va-t-il?" Nicolette asked in her native French tongue as she eased past the wall her sons unwittingly created with their tall bodies. She stepped in front of the surgeon.

"She asked if he was okay," Gabe supplied.

Nicolette offered the hint of an apologetic smile. "I'm sorry. It's hard to think straight with my love on a table with his chest open, Dr. Taha," she said.

The doctor's smile was far brighter. "The surgery went well. His chest is stitched shut and his heart will be better in time," she said, making eye contact with every last one of them. "He's in Recovery and then will be moved to ICU for a few days."

The relief they all felt was palpable.

Nicolette covered her face with both hands and wept.

Lincoln welcomed Bobbie's arms around his waist as he settled his chin atop her head.

Phillip Junior sank onto a seat as if his legs gave out beneath him. Raquel rushed to his side.

Sean clapped Lucas's back soundly as their baby brother kept nodding as if afraid to stop and change the prognosis.

Cole's expression was stoic, but his eyes revealed the truth of his concern for the father with whom he used to be constantly at odds. Jillian gathered his hands in hers and raised them to press kisses to the backs of them.

Gabe and Monica clung to each other.

Long after the doctor left them, everyone reclaimed their seats and allowed themselves to smile again.

"À la nourriture. À la vie. À l'amour," Nicolette said in her native tongue as she moved to each of the brothers to squeeze their hand.

It was her favorite saying. To food. To life. To love.

It was painted on the wall above all of her stoves—personal and professional—and was branded on all Cress, INC. cookware, stationery, magazines, online presences and TV shows.

"À la nourriture. À la vie. À l'amour," they all repeated in unison.

All at once, email notifications began to sound off.

Bzzzzzz.

Ding.

Bzzzzzz.

Beep.

Boop.

You got mail!

Nicolette and the other brothers pulled out their phones. "Google alert," she said.

"Do not become this," she whispered to him.

"Never," he swore.

The Cress family—world-renowned chefs and owners of a massive culinary empire—are back in the spotlight and this time it's the biggest star. None other than celebrity chef, A-lister, ladies' man and frequent party attendee Sean Cress. And this one is a doozy—

All eyes landed on Sean.

Nicolette's blue eyes were frigid as she cut Sean to the quick with a lethal stare. "What have you done?" she snapped.

Sean offered a weak smile and one-shoulder shrug.

Lincoln and Bobbie shared a long look before he leaned over to press a kiss to her temple. "You sure you want to be in *this* family," he spoke into her ear, his tone slightly bemused.

Bobbie shivered in awareness from his mouth brushing against her earlobe. "With you by my side? Absolutely," she assured him, before turning her head to capture his mouth with a kiss filled with the promise of lasting love.

* * * * *

WE HOPE YOU ENJOYED
THIS BOOK FROM

DESIRE

*Luxury, scandal, desire—welcome to
the lives of the American elite.*

Be transported to the worlds of oil barons, family dynasties,
moguls and celebrities. Get ready for juicy plot twists,
delicious sensuality and intriguing scandal.

6 NEW BOOKS AVAILABLE EVERY MONTH!

#2887 RIVALRY AT PLAY

Texas Cattleman's Club: Ranchers and Rivals
by Nadine Gonzalez

Attorney Alexandra Lattimore isn't looking for love. She's home to help her family—and to escape problems at work. But sparks with former rival Jackson Strom are too hot to resist. Will her secrets keep them from rewriting their past?

#2888 THEIR MARRIAGE BARGAIN

Dynasties: Tech Tycoons • by Shannon McKenna

If biotech tycoon Caleb Moss isn't married soon, he'll lose control of the family company. Ex Tilda Riley's unexpected return could solve his marriage bind—in name only. But can this convenient arrangement withstand the heat between them?

#2889 A COLORADO CLAIM

Return to Catamount • by Joanne Rock

Returning home to defend her inheritance, Lark Barclay is surprised to see her ex-husband, rancher Gibson Vaughn. And Gibson proves hard to ignore. She's out to claim her land, but will he reclaim her heart?

#2890 CROSSING TWO LITTLE LINES

by Joss Wood

When heiress Jamie Bacall and blue-collar billionaire Rowan Cowper meet in an elevator, a hot, no-strings fling ensues. But when Jamie learns she's pregnant, will their relationship cross the line into something more?

#2891 THE NANNY GAME

The Eddington Heirs • by Zuri Day

Running his family's empire is a full-time job, so when a baby is dropped off at his estate, Desmond Eddington needs nanny Ivy Campbell. Escaping painful pasts, neither is open to love, but it's impossible to ignore their attraction...

#2892 BLAME IT ON VEGAS

Bad Billionaires • by Kira Sinclair

Avid card shark Luca Kilpatrick hasn't returned to the casino since Annalise Mercado's family accused him of cheating. But now he's the only one who can catch a thief—if he can resist the chemistry that's too strong to deny...

Finding his father's assistant at an underground fight club, playboy Mason Kane realizes he isn't the only one leading a double life. So he offers Charlotte Westbrook a whirlwind Riviera fling to help her loosen up, but it could cost her job and her heart...

Read on for a sneak peek at
Secret Lives After Hours
by Cynthia St. Aubin

They stood facing each other, the summer heat still radiating up from the sidewalk, the sultry breath of a coming storm sifting through their hair.

Now.

Now was the moment where she would pull out her phone, bring up the ride app. Bid him good-night. If she did this, the past three hours could be bundled into a box neither of them would ever have to open again. He might smile at her secretly every now and then, wink at her in acknowledgment, but that would be the end of it.

If she left now.

"Come up," Mason said.

It wasn't a question. It wasn't even an invitation.

It was an answer.

An answer to her own admission in the elevator. That she liked looking at him. That she could look at him more if she wanted.

That he wanted her to.

"Okay," Charlotte said.

Don't miss what happens next in…
Secret Lives After Hours *by Cynthia St. Aubin,*
the next book in The Kane Heirs series!
Available August 2022 wherever
Harlequin Desire books and ebooks are sold.

Harlequin.com

Get 4 FREE REWARDS!

We'll send you 2 FREE Books plus 2 FREE Mystery Gifts.

FREE Value Over **$20**

Both the **Harlequin® Desire** and **Harlequin Presents®** series feature compelling novels filled with passion, sensuality and intriguing scandals.

Love Harlequin romance?

DISCOVER.

Be the first to find out about promotions, news and exclusive content!

f Facebook.com/HarlequinBooks

𝕏 Twitter.com/HarlequinBooks

⊙ Instagram.com/HarlequinBooks

ⓟ Pinterest.com/HarlequinBooks

You Tube YouTube.com/HarlequinBooks

ReaderService.com

EXPLORE.

Sign up for the Harlequin e-newsletter and download a free book from any series at
TryHarlequin.com

CONNECT.

Join our Harlequin community to share your thoughts and connect with other romance readers!
Facebook.com/groups/HarlequinConnection

HARLEQUIN

Heartfelt or thrilling, passionate or uplifting—Harlequin is more than just happily-ever-after.

With twelve different series to choose from and new books available every month, you are sure to find stories that will move you, uplift you, inspire and delight you.

HNEWS2021